PATRICK CAVANAUGH

In Plain Sight

A Reconstruction Era Tale of Greed and Desire

First edition

ISBN (paperback): 979-8-9929769-0-8
ISBN (hardcover): 979-8-9929769-2-2

Editing by Christy Koury
Cover art by Rosenbaum Creative
Illustration by John Eden

This book was professionally typeset on Reedsy.
Find out more at reedsy.com

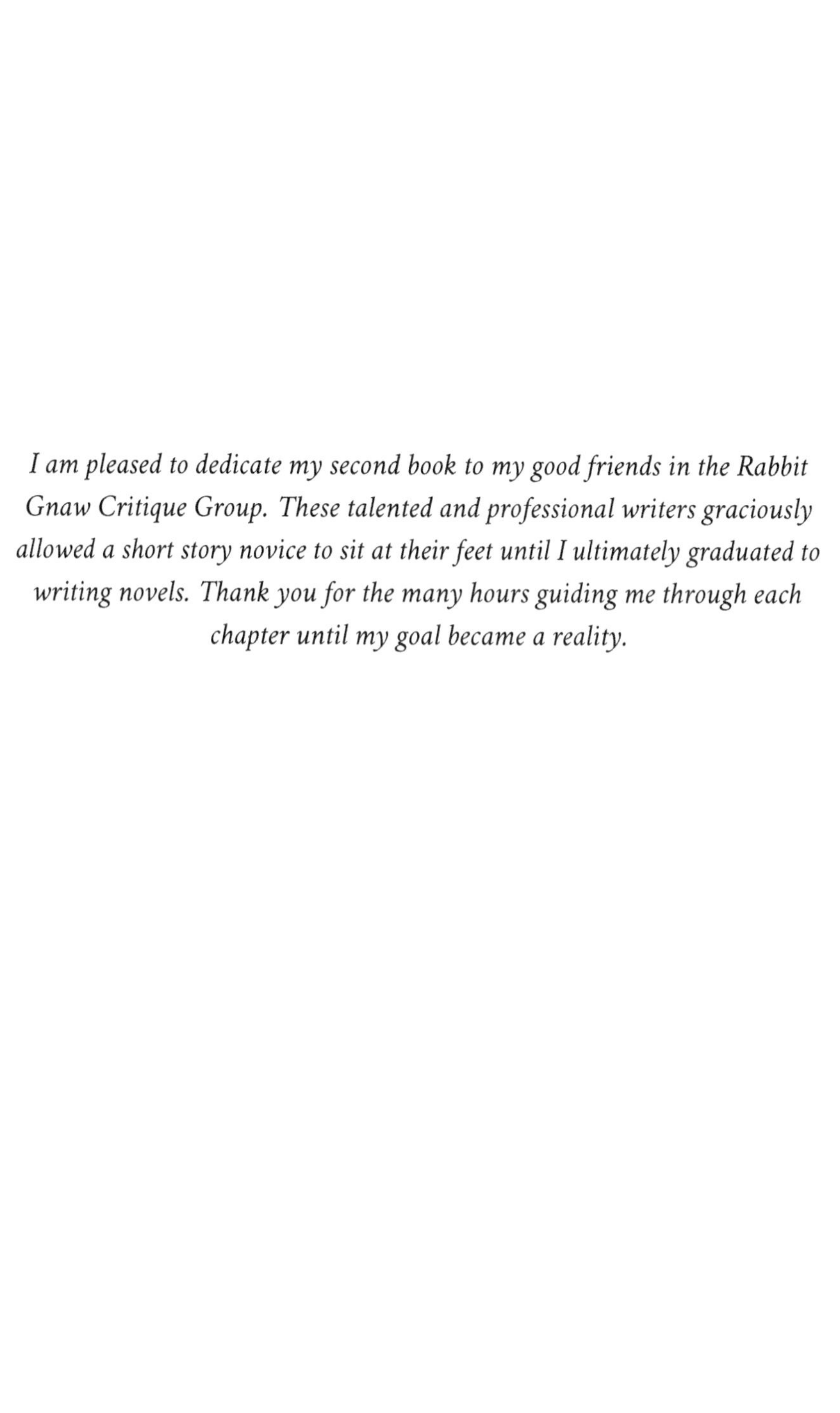

I am pleased to dedicate my second book to my good friends in the Rabbit Gnaw Critique Group. These talented and professional writers graciously allowed a short story novice to sit at their feet until I ultimately graduated to writing novels. Thank you for the many hours guiding me through each chapter until my goal became a reality.

Contents

Preface

This book is a sequel to *Beneath the Quince Bush*, a story about Colonel and Jetta Whittlesey, owners of Heartwood Plantation near Savannah, Georgia, during the Civil War of 1861. While Hugh Whittlesey serves with the Georgia engineers, Heartwood is ravaged by General Sherman during his infamous "March to the Sea," and Jetta is assaulted by the leader of the looters.

In Plain Sight picks up the story during the Reconstruction period that began in 1865. Jetta is now a widow, struggling with the failed cotton crops, the emancipation of her former slaves and the pending sale of her plantation to satisfy taxes. She is stunned by the sudden appearance of her former attacker with an unwanted offer of assistance and its frightful cost. However, even his murder does not relieve her precarious future.

1

Chapter One: April 3, 1870: Hide and Seek

D inky Dillon's bar was located in Chicago's Mount Greenwood area on the south side of the city. It was unfriendly, dark and dirty with an oppressively low ceiling and a few uncomfortable booths along one wall. It was not a very appealing place to enjoy your pint of Guinness, unless you were a Chicago policeman. The city's finest regularly migrated there in successive waves after their shifts. They leaned on the long mahogany bar, munched on the free pig's knuckles or briny hard-boiled eggs from the big glass jars, smoked their cigars and drank their whiskey neat. The two favorite topics of conversation were women and crime, and the two subjects were generally related.

Thomas Duckett, a young investigator for the Pinkerton National Detective Agency, sat alone in one of the cramped booths, squinting his eyes in the flickering light of a candle and reading for the third time the story posted on the front page of yesterday's newspaper.

Missing Millionaire

AP Chicago, Illinois, April 2, 1870

Chicago police announced today that they are investigating the sudden disappearance of wealthy Chicago businessman, Terrance Rourke, age 42. Mr. Rourke was last seen by his wife Isabelle when he left for work on the morning of April 1st. His secretary and business associates confirmed that he failed to arrive at his office that day.

Mr. Rourke is the owner of a chain of department stores in the Midwest with its headquarters in the flagship store on Halstead Avenue in Chicago. He also has extensive investments in banking and insurance operations in the city.

Mr. Rourke's long-time business partner, Seymour Weekes, professed to be mystified by his associate's disappearance and suggested the possibility of foul play.

Financial sources who declined to be named said that the Rourke business empire was in "absolutely fabulous" financial condition. However, they had been baffled by some of his recent actions, whereby he liquidated about a third of his holdings to cash, the location of which has not been determined.

Mr. Rourke's law firm, Strudwick & Kemp, refused to comment on a rumor that he had also recently brought his legal affairs up to date.

Adding to the mystery was a report of a business acquaintance who claimed he saw Mr. Rourke at the train station in Atlanta, Georgia shortly after his disappearance. He said that Mr. Rourke's appearance was quite changed, as he was clean-shaven and wore eyeglasses. When the source greeted Mr. Rourke by name, the man claimed that he was mistaken and excused himself because of an appointment.

Mr. Rourke served in the Union Army for sixteen years and was a decorated veteran of the Civil War, having fought in battles in Chattanooga, Atlanta and in General William Sherman's "March to the Sea" across Georgia.

Anyone having any knowledge of Mr. Rourke's disappearance is urged to contact the Chicago Police Department.

***

Duckett put down the paper and leaned back in the booth, his mind racing back to an interview he had with a client back in early February. The man had called the Pinkerton office and said he wanted to hire one of their top investigators for some research on a private matter of some importance. The client refused to give his name and insisted the interview had to take place in a private suite of a local hotel. Duckett had attempted to find the client's name by identifying himself to the room clerk as Parker Kellogg, an attorney from the prestigious Chicago firm of Strudwick & Kemp only to discover later that the client was registered under a false name.

When he had knocked on the designated room's door, a voice ordered him to come in, but when he entered, he found himself blinded by two spotlights. A tall screen hid the client. "Pick up the envelope on the chair and sit down," the voice said. "Then open the envelope."

Duckett was surprised to discover he held five thousand dollars in his hand. He started to comment, but the voice interrupted him. "Be quiet and listen, Mr. Duckett. I have had you investigated, and I know more about you than your own mother does. You served three years as a policeman and had a good record. You are resourceful and intelligent. Pinkerton hired you as an investigator, and you are now one of their top men. People like you and trust you. You are intensely ambitious, but you do not let it show.

"The money in your hand is the first payment for a private investigation. If you perform the investigation successfully, there will be another payment of five thousand dollars.

"You told the desk clerk that you are an employee of Strudwick & Kemp. You even had the embossed card to prove it! What a nice touch," the voice mocked.

"I want you to travel to Savannah, Georgia to investigate a nearby plantation called Heartwood, owned by the Whittlesey family. You can pose as an attorney working for a Chicago consortium of businessmen interested in buying promising properties in the area. Find out everything you can about the property, physically and financially. I also want a thorough report on the owners."

The voice now took a chilling edge. "You are curious, Mr. Duckett, and you are ambitious. That is a dangerous combination. If you try to identify me or pursue any of the information you have uncovered, you will have a lethal accident. Do I make myself clear, Mr. Duckett?"

Duckett swallowed with difficulty. "Yes, sir," he said.

***

He shifted position in the booth and took a long swallow of his beer. Why did his mysterious client remind him of Terrance Rourke, the man in the paper? His client was obviously wealthy, intelligent and dangerous. He had an interest in some property in Georgia. The missing man in the paper was also rich and had made a flawless disappearance, except for a chance sighting in the Atlanta railroad terminal.

Duckett needed more information, and he knew where he could get it. Thomas Healy was a seasoned detective with the Chicago police who had befriended Duckett during his time on the force. He had a wide circle of informants on both sides of the law. A burly, red-haired Irishman with a hair-trigger temper, he expected a quick and truthful response to his questions, and he generally got it. Healy made a daily appearance at Dinky's bar after his shift. His favorite drink was a boilermaker, a shot glass of Tullamore Dew gently lowered into a cold mug of draft beer. As if on cue, a gaggle of noisy policemen burst through the doors of the saloon, with Healy in the forefront.

"Healy! Over here!" called Duckett.

The big man pointed a finger at the barman and then swaggered over to the booth where Duckett sat and squeezed his large body into the opposite seat. "Well, well! If it isn't the young man from Pinkerton!

What would you be doin' down here with us commoners, laddie-buck?"

He looked up and beamed when the waiter arrived with his drink. "Ah, would you just look at that, now! All those lovely little bubbles swimmin' up to the foam!" He took a long, appreciative swallow, then set the glass down and squinted at his young friend.

"I'm guessing you want some information, am I right?"

Duckett passed him the article he had been reading. "What do you know about this case?" he asked.

"I know all the latest gossip, which I will tell you for the price of payin' for me drinks. I also know all the good information we have, but that will be a wee bit more costly." He rubbed his thumb and first finger together suggestively.

Duckett sighed and reached for his billfold. He extracted two fifty-dollar bills and pushed them over to Healy.

"Splendid!" said the big man. "Now, let's see how much you remember of what I taught you. What's your first question?"

"Do you think Terrance Rourke is alive or dead?"

"Come on, laddie! What do you think?"

Duckett thought for a moment. "The witness in the rail station knew him well, and he is convinced it was Rourke. His banker knew he had cashed in on one third of his business, but I doubt he would tell anyone, so no one knew about the money, which would be the main reason to kill him."

"And who else has reason to do him in?"

Duckett shrugged. "His business partner, Weekes?"

"Negative, and if you ever met him, you would know he's a shifty fella' but not somebody who would ever murder anyone. Besides, he's now sittin' in the catbird seat and runnin' the whole show, all six million dollars' worth."

Duckett was silent for a minute while he absorbed that news. If Rourke took away a third of his fortune and he left six million dollars, he left with three million in cash! "Any business enemies around the city that he ran over?"

Healy shook his head. "Plenty he outsmarted, but that's as far as it went."

"What did he do in the war?"

Healy reached out a big hand and patted his friend gently on one check. "Now you are startin' to think like a detective. Sergeant Terrance Rourke was a true warrior and won a medal for bravery in battle, but he also had a reputation for taking care of himself first. He fought in battles from Chattanooga to Columbia, South Carolina and only quit when he was wounded. Durin' General Sherman's march, he wuz one of Sherman's "bummers" who raided plantations for food and fodder for the army. Rumor had it they also helped themselves to silver and jewelry, too, even though Sherman strictly forbade that kinda thing. And of course, Rourke burned down lots of plantations if there was any action against Sherman's troops in the area, like settin' mines in the roads. There must be lots of southern Rebs who would like to get their hands on Sergeant Terrance Rourke, even today."

Duckett considered that for a moment then shook his head. 'I can see them coming after Sherman after the war was over. He would be a lot easier to find, and they knew who was in charge. But trying to find the name and whereabouts of some sergeant? That's like a needle in the haystack."

Healy shrugged. "Who's your best suspect, then?"

"What about his wife?"

Healy shook his head. "As fine a woman as I ever saw. Cryin' her heart out. Calls the station every day to see if we have any news. Three young daughters, fine house, no money worries at all.

"Now, if you ask me, I don't think they had any big love affair, 'specially on Rourke's part. Separate bedrooms, no public show of affection, none of that, but kindness and respect, yes. And Rourke was never seen foolin' around with any of Chicago's ladies of the night."

Duckett raised his hands in frustration. "I give up! What's your take on the situation?"

Healy took another long swallow of his drink and then wiped his lips with the back of his hand. "This is a man who has everythin.' He's in good health, owns several thrivin' businesses, big bucks in the bank, nice family, plenty of power and respect and he's in his early forties." He shook his forefinger at his young friend. "And you know what?" He leaned closer to Duckett. "He's bored! Bored to tears! He needs another challenge, he does!

"And one more thing. Our boy is at that age where men start to get that 'ole itch in their britches. They get to dreamin' about some lovely lass they knew when they were younger. You put that itch in the britches alongside of boredom when they wakes up every mornin' and they are goin' to do something stupid."

"Somebody he met in the war?" asked Duckett.

Healy shrugged. "Why not? I wuz in that bitchin' war! Scared shitless most of the time! No time to be bored. And when it was quiet, which was not very often, every woman looked good, even the ugly ones."

"I buy the bored part, that I understand. But if Rourke was looting plantations and burning them down, what southern woman would fall for a man like that? She would hate his guts!"

"You remember this, my young friend," said the big man. "For every foot there's a sock!" Healy drained his boilermaker, thumped the empty glass on the table, and waved to the bartender.

"One last question, Healy. Are there any little interesting facts that did not come out in the newspaper?"

"I talked to all the servants in the house and they all noticed somethin' different. They said he was in a very good humor the week before he disappeared."

"So, whatever he had planned, he looked forward to it with pleasure."

"Yes indeed! Like gettin' together with a sweet dolly he hadn't seen in a long time."

"Any other clues about the money?"

"He took the money in cash. Why in hell would he do that? A check or draft is easier and weighs a ton less, but when he goes to cash it he has to identify himself and people will find out where he has settled."

"Got it," said Duckett. "One last thing. Isn't anyone talking about a reward?"

"No, and you can bet your boots there ain't gonna be one! Way he left was like darin' folks to come after him! But tell me somethin'. Who's askin' the questions here, you or Pinkerton? Are they offering their services to find Rourke, or is a certain young man dreamin' about how he can get his hands on all that money?" Healy leaned across the table until his face was right up to Duckett's. "Maybe this young man thinks he knows when Rourke is hidin' and offers to keep his secret in exchange for a nice piece of that three million bucks? If that's the case, son, listen to me and listen good: Terrance Rourke is a damn sight smarter than you and even me, and he ain't afraid of anybody on earth! He got medals in the war for killin' people 'cause he was damn good at it! If you tangle with him, he will leave you lyin' in some alley with a hole in your head!

"Ah, thankee kindly!" he continued as a fresh drink thumped down on the table. He took a long pull and wiped his lips with his cuff. "Lemme tell you a story 'bout Rourke. Two years ago, he and his wife came outta a restaurant where a big fella with a knife tole' him to hand over his money. Rourke had a fancy cane with a gold handle. He broke the man's hand so that he dropped the knife, hit him in the mouth an' broke four teeth, then clubbed him behind the ear. Half hour later when the police showed up, fella was still out cold." Healy pointed a finger at his friend. "That's the kind of man you be dealin' with, boy-o."

When Duckett finally left the darkened bar, he saw a horse-drawn tram passing on the other side of the road. He waved his arm, whistled, and sprinted through the traffic to pull himself on board. He picked an empty seat in the back and sat back to think about what he had learned. It was too bad about the reward, but he would have had to share that with Pinkerton, and that was just as dangerous as demanding a big slice from Rourke himself. What about getting a partner with no contacts to Rourke to make the demand? That was a lot safer, but suppose the man took the money and ran? Duckett sighed and shook his head. Crime was complicated.

2

Chapter Two: Fear and Remorse

Six years earlier, in 1864, General William Tecumseh Sherman had subdued the city of Atlanta, calling it a "military center" and ordering all residents to be evacuated. Sherman prepared his sixty thousand troops to push aside a scant three thousand men available in Georgia and to concentrate on the threat on the Atlantic Ocean only three hundred miles away.

Considering Georgia civilians "lines of supply," Sherman established cadres of trained men who knew how to strip a plantation clean of food, fodder and laborers and quickly rejoin their troops. One such man was Sergeant Terrance Rourke of the Seventh Illinois Mounted Cavalry. He and his men were all specially trained as "bummers," responsible for keeping Sherman's men filled daily with food and forage.

Most of the officers knew that Rourke was one of the best shots in the army—on horseback or on the ground. What the officers did not know about Rourke was that he was very competent in another job besides military service and never let one hinder the other. After the bummers confiscated every item of service to their soldiers, they quickly began to steal anything Rourke wanted for himself: money, jewelry, clothing—anything of mobile value that could easily be sent back home by rail.

Meanwhile, in Chicago's rail center, Rourke had a good military man called Major Weekes who could somehow move equipment around like magic. Together, the two of them were amassing a fortune in Rourke's name.

In December of 1864, Rourke's commander, Colonel Hitchens was enraged by the loss of one of his head sergeants to a land mine near Heartwood Plantation, the home of Jetta Whittlesey and Colonel Champion Whittlesey, who was absent defending his country. In his fury, Hitchens ordered his bummers to "Pick this place clean and burn it to the ground."

While raiding Heartwood Plantation, Rourke found himself impressed by Jetta Whittlesey, who stood up to him defiantly. As Rourke's men ransacked the plantation, the sergeant asked her to divulge where she had hidden her valuables, but she refused to tell him. In response, Rourke ordered his men to hang Jubal, Jetta's Negro overseer, from a nearby oak tree, where they left him to choke and kick until Jetta begged for his release. As her faithful servant lay on the ground retching, Jetta led Rourke to the quince bush under which all her valuables were hidden. When he admired her ruby necklace, Champion's last gift, she pleaded with him to leave it, but he refused. She called him a coward, preying on defenseless women, and he grabbed her arm, dragged her back to the plantation house and…

After taking her family fortune and more, Rourke rode away, leaving Jetta defeated. A few weeks later, Jetta received the news that her husband, Champion, had been killed in action.

***

Sergeant Terrance Rourke was lucky for the rest of the war. Many would say he was extremely lucky. He amassed a hoard of stolen goods. After he was wounded and discharged from the army, he returned to

Chicago where he and his partner Weekes opened dry goods stores called Rourke's Emporiums. There, one could buy, amongst other things, fine stolen goods at a great price.

As his fortune grew, Rourke moved into Chicago society, marrying a well-bred woman who bore him three daughters whom he treated well. However, he never forgot Jetta Whittlesey. In the end, it was his memory of her that led him to hire a private investigator to explore her plight and, ultimately, to abandon his Chicago life, assume a new identity and travel to Heartwood Plantation again to pursue a life with Jetta and his bastard son.

Unfortunately, that was the end of the good luck of Sergeant Rourke and the beginning of his future under the quince bush.

***

In April of 1870, the early sunshine was kind to the Heartwood Plantation. It was difficult to see the neat patches on the steep roof, the faded paint on the sides of the house, and the various colors of different bricks. There were no men or women scurrying around the tall home to begin the day.

At the wide back porch, Jubal, carefully closed the door and carried a heavy bundle on his right shoulder. He reached down with his left hand and picked up an old shovel, then began to walk slowly down the chipped steps. Jetta stepped out onto the porch behind him. Before Jubal stretched brick terraces with lush plants growing at each side. He stopped at a tall quince bush on the right side, taller than several others, and carefully laid his bundle on the wet grass. One of the canvas bindings broke loose at the far end, releasing the head of Rourke, his eyes wildly open, his teeth grimacing, and blood trickling down his neck.

Jubal assessed the object for a moment, picked it up carefully, and stuffed it back into the canvas wrapping.

He prodded the ground at the root of the quince bush thoughtfully, remembering the day when it was rudely chopped open by Rourke's diggers to claim Jetta's hidden property. Jubal replanted the area a week later. He shook his head ruefully and began to dig the bush carefully up again. When the hole was deep enough, he pushed the body in and replaced the quince bush over it.

Wrapped in a dark cape, the wind blowing her black hair across her face, Jetta held a lantern high while Jubal finished his grisly work. Together they made their silent way back to the darkened plantation house.

"He horse an' buggy," said Jubal, pointing to the rig behind the plantation house.

"Oh!" said Jetta. "He must have rented it from Mr. Pollitt in Pembroke. Oh, God! What if he told Pollitt where he was going!"

Jubal shook his head once. "This man not talk much."

"We have to return it immediately so it will appear that he left!"

'I wake my son, Toby. He follow me in de wagon when I drives back to town."

"But someone might see you!"

"Too dark. I leaves the wagon outside town, horses go back to de stable themselves." he explained. He silently handed her a dark leather breast wallet.

"His clothes! I forgot his clothes! I have to take them from his room before Tiny cleans it in the morning."

"When I gets back, we clean your room and I burn de clothes." He was silent a moment, then asked, "You sleep dere?"

"Can I sleep in the room I shared so happily with my late husband? Yes!" she said fiercely. Holding the lantern high, Jetta climbed the back steps and entered the silent house. She quickly went up the stairs and entered the guest room where Rourke had stayed. Immediately she was aware of the cloying smell of an eau de cologne and cigar smoke.

"Bah!" she exclaimed and threw a window open. She put her lantern on a bureau and turned up the light, then opened the bottom drawer to extract a sheet which she spread on the bed. There was a man's shaving kit and a leather cigar holder on top of the bureau which she put on the sheet and then turned her attention to the first drawer, which yielded two fine shirts with detachable collars, silk underwear that surprised her, socks and cravats and a rolled-up newspaper, all of which she put on the bed.

All the other drawers were empty.

Jetta opened the door to the chifforobe and saw a brown tweed suit, a man's trilby hat, a light overcoat and a sturdy pair of men's shoes. An inner pocket of the suit contained a gold pen. She put it all on the sheet on the bed.

Two items remained in the chifforobe, a man's small leather bag with straps and a large brown portmanteau with a leather handle. She put the bag on the bed and opened it. It was empty except for a box of bullets, a small box of imported cigars and a large box of matches, all of which she added to the pile on the bed.

The bullets reminded Jetta of something, and she lifted the candle off the bureau and returned to her bedroom. She took a sharp intake of breath when she saw the small rug at the entrance soaked with coalescing blood that had fanned across her bedroom floor. Biting her lip hard, she lowered the lantern and searched the floor until she saw a glint of metal from the small derringer Rourke had attempted to reach before Jubal's cane knife cut his throat. As she reached down to pick up the gun, she saw another object lying under her bed. Kneeling on the floor she stretched out her arm and picked up the familiar gold and ruby necklace that Champion had given her on his last leave from the army.

"Oh!" she exclaimed, clutching it to her breast, as she remembered the last time she had seen it. The memory caused her to break out in racking sobs and she put her head on her bed as she knelt on the hard floor.

Jetta suddenly snapped out of her reverie and stood up, put the necklace and the gun in a drawer in her bedroom and returned to Rourke's room to finish her work. She tried to lift the remaining portmanteau and was surprised at its weight. A small lock prevented her from opening the zipper, but she found the key in a fold in Rourke's wallet.

She was shocked to see the contents: money! Stack after stack of money, crisp federal greenbacks bound together with paper bands marked with the logo of the First Federal Bank of Chicago. Rourke had been sincere in his offer to pay Heartwood's debts and to pay for her son Paul's education if, in return, Jetta would eventually consider his hand in marriage. But she had emphatically rejected his proposal, sending Jubal with his cane knife as her messenger. Rourke was gone, but here sat his money. Money that could save Heartwood from a tax sale. Money that could pay her debts to her factor in Savannah. Money that could repair her roof and clear the irrigation ditches. Money that could... No, No! The money was not hers! But whose was it? She covered her eyes in despair. She needed help and advice. Whom could she turn to?

∗∗∗

"Jetta, my dear! I came as soon as I could! How can I help you?" asked Judge Abner Huckabee as he stood at her front door. He wore his usual dark suit and removed his hat to reveal a full head of white hair parted neatly in the center.

Jetta flung her arms around her oldest friend.

"Oh, Judge! "I am in terrible trouble! I have had a man killed! I had

Jubal kill him!" she said.

He put his arm around her and led her inside to a small love seat and sat down beside her, dabbing at her eyes with a silk handkerchief. He lifted up her chin and said, "There is no doubt in my mind that if you had someone killed, that person deserved it! Now tell me how it happened."

Jetta bit her lip and then began. "You know about the raid on Heartwood by Sherman's bummers in December of 1864." She shook her head. "But I never told you the whole story." She recounted how Rourke had hung Jubal from a tree branch until she had confided where she had hidden her silver and jewelry under a quince bush.

"He stood there admiring the ruby necklace Champion had given me on his last leave. I begged him not to take it, but he did. Then he asked me if I had hidden any more valuables!" She shook her head violently.

"I was infuriated! I called him a coward, a man who made war on defenseless women and innocent slaves! I called him the devil incarnate!

"He called for a pine torch and then grabbed me by my arm, dragging me into the house and ordering everyone else outside. He told me he was going to introduce me to the devil I had compared him to and said if I did not consent to spend the night with him in my bedroom, he would burn Heartwood to the ground and carry Jubal away to work on removing land mines from the road." She shuddered and then looked directly at her friend.

Her voice sank to a whisper. "He made his soldiers stay over that night and then took me to my bridal bed. I lay there with my eyes closed and unmoving, repulsed by the smell of him while he assaulted me. When I awoke, he was gone." Her face was white and her eyes had a haunted look.

The judge's face was flushed with anger. "My dear girl! What a terrible thing you have endured! You should have reported him to his superiors! Sherman has hanged men for less!"

Jetta bowed her head. "I am partly responsible. I taunted him and questioned his courage. Champion told me to be circumspect, even if it meant losing the plantation, but I did not control my anger. I was afraid that if Champion found out what had happened, he would desert the army and pursue the man until he killed him or was killed himself. I would keep what happened to me a secret, a very dark secret." She shook her head slowly. "And then Champion died, and I found that I was pregnant."

The judge's eyes widened in shock. "Paul?" he asked, incredulously.

"Yes, my beloved Paul," she admitted. "But I did not love him, at first. To me he was the spawn of that devil, Rourke!" She broke out in tears again. "I actually tried to smother him when he was first born! But he pursued me with his love until I gave him mine." She stood suddenly and looked out the window, her arms crossed.

"And then that devil shows up again! Now he has the dress and the manners of a gentleman! He is so contrite about what happened! How he wishes we could have met under different circumstances! But he will make it up to me! He will pay my debts, restore Heartwood to its former glory, give 'his' son the finest education available! He will be my advisor, my manager, until he has earned my respect and yes, my love!" she spat out the word. "And then? Why, we will marry and live happily together, man and wife.

"The most terrifying part of his plan was his intention to raise Paul to be the son he had always wanted! I could never, never allow that to happen! I pretended to consider his offer and told him I would give him my final answer that evening in my bedroom. When he entered my bedroom that evening, Jubal was waiting for him."

The judge was dumbfounded by what he had heard. "Where is the body, Jetta?"

She gave a bitter laugh. "He is in a fitting place, Judge! Beneath the same quince bush his men dug up so rudely to steal my silver and jewelry."

The judge bowed his head and rubbed his brow with his hand.

"I am having difficulty absorbing all of this, my dear."

"Unfortunately, there is more, Judge." She walked to a nearby table, picked up a folded newspaper and offered it to her old friend. "I found this in his room."

The judge looked at the photograph in the heading and then looked up at her. "This is the man, Rourke?"

"It is, the way he looked before shaving off his beard."

The judge read the article carefully, frowning from time to time. When he finally put it down, he said, "Jetta this man has amassed a considerable fortune! And he has gone to great effort to assure that no one will ever discover where he has gone. That may be to your advantage."

Jetta shook her head. "Unfortunately, I think there may be one person who knows. Rourke knew too many details about my finances and my personal life. I do not believe he was in any position to collect this information himself, so I believe he hired some sort of professional to come here and spy on me. Let me show you something." She rose and returned a few minutes later with a letter.

"This is the letter Rourke used to arrange his appointment with me. He identifies himself as Parker Kellogg from the Chicago firm of Strudwick and Kemp, representing certain businessmen who were interested in investing in Heartwood. In March of this year, I received a letter from Kellogg saying he was visiting the Savannah area looking for plantations in which to invest money. I know he came here because he introduced himself to a friend of mine, Abigail Simpson. She was very disappointed when he left without saying goodbye."

"Did you say his name was Parker Kellogg? I know the man! He called on me asking for information on local plantations that could be purchased! But he was a young man and looked nothing like this man in the paper!" The judge was visibly upset.

"So, we know at least one person knows of Rourke's plan to resettle here at Heartwood," concluded Jetta.

The judge rose to his feet and began pacing the room.

"Think carefully, my dear. How many people at Heartwood knew of a man who said he was Parker Kellogg?"

"Well, there was me, of course, and Jubal. Tiny, my maid. Oh! And Paul! He made quite an impression on Paul!"

"Probably some other Negros as well. Hmm." His face suddenly brightened.

"Here is what we will do, my dear! If anyone comes here and claims that Terrance Rourke came here, you will deny it. The only guest you have had recently is a man called Parker Kellogg, a much younger man known by two friends of yours! And you probably have his card to prove you are telling the truth."

"Indeed, I do!"

"Good!" The judge kept walking and rubbing his hands together. "But you turned him away, didn't you, Jetta?"

"I did?" she asked, faintly.

"Yes, you did!" he said vehemently. "And the reason was… was… Ah ha! The reason was you had already accepted another offer from another group of investors in… in…Philadelphia! And they loaned you this!" He swooped down on the bag of money and held it aloft. "They loaned you…?" He looked at her quizzically.

"Two hundred and fifty thousand dollars."

"They loaned you two hundred and fifty thousand dollars at five percent interest!"

"Judge, that money is not mine, and I want no part of it."

He sat down in his chair and pulled it closer to her.

"My dear, you have no alternative. If you cannot pay the taxes due this month, some carpetbagger will own Heartwood for the paltry sum of ten thousand dollars. Or John Flannery's company, your factor, will own it for what you owe them. Do not allow that to happen! This money is a gift from God! Accept it and give thanks."

"But people will say I had Rourke killed for his money," she said.

"No, the people who know you will not believe such slander. And what others think is of no consequence." He rose from his chair and reached for his hat.

"I will begin work immediately on your so-called contract with the investors in Philadelphia. It will specify that I am their agent in this enterprise, and I will deposit the money with one of the federal banks in Savannah. You will be able to cash checks on that account, signed by you and me. You will pay the monthly interest payments from the account as well, payable to me as agent and I will cash them and give you the money back."

Jetta shook her head in dismay. "Judge, you will be breaking the law for my sake!"

"Several laws, my dear, but for a good cause. I will return after I have finished the agreement."

***

When Judge Huckabee arrived home, he went immediately to his study, sat at his desk and searched until he found his book of addresses. He found the address in Philadelphia where his nephew Nathan practiced law. He had provided the young man with the funds he needed to get his law degree, and had no qualms about asking him for assistance.

April 7, 1870

My dear nephew:
I need your assistance on a very important matter, and unfortunately, time

is short.

You must create for me a sham Philadelphia corporation named Mainline Associates to pose as a group of wealthy businessmen interested in investing in southern plantations and other facilities in the South. This entity should have a legitimate charter, but will have no function. You personally should be listed as the Secretary-Treasurer of this corporation.

I suspect you will be approached by someone who wants to verify the existence of this entity and whether it has business interests in Georgia. Your response should be that the corporation does not reveal any information about its functions, but you should make every effort to discover the identity of the person making the inquiry.

Thank you for your help, and may God Bless You!

Uncle Abner

***

The judge addressed an envelope and put the letter to one side. He lifted the top on his cigar humidor and carefully selected his first cigar of the day. He sniffed it appreciatively, then opened the top drawer of his desk and picked up a small pen knife, which he used to cut off the end. He struck a sulphur match and ignited the cigar, puffing until the end glowed red. He then leaned back in his chair to consider his next move.

The cigar was about half gone and the room fragrant with tobacco aroma when the judge decided on his next step. He pulled another sheet of paper from a drawer and began to write.

April 7, 1870

Thornton Doubleday, President

National Bank of Savannah
Savannah, Georgia

Dear Thornton:

I have been contacted by Mainline Associates of Philadelphia, a group of investors, to be their agent with respect to a contract with Mrs. Champion Whittlesey, owner of Heartwood plantation, whereby they would invest a sizable sum of money in the property secured by a first mortgage. The money would be deposited in your bank at an agreed rate of interest and distributed to Mrs. Whittlesey as needed by checks signed by me.

Please advise when it would be convenient for you to meet with Mrs. Whittlesey and me.

Yours truly,
Abner Huckabee

The judge sealed the letter in an envelope and put it to one side. He had a nagging feeling he had forgotten something. Of course! A mortgage! There had to be a mortgage! He rummaged around in his desk until he found a standard form and filled in the spaces, establishing a mortgage on the Heartwood property as collateral for the loan from the mock corporation to Jetta Whittlesey. He would file the form with the clerk of the court in the nearby town of Pembroke, Georgia. The news of such an event would spread like wildfire in the local legal community.

The judge rose from his desk and walked down the hall to his bedroom. He sat on a stool and pulled off his shoes, rubbed his feet and pulled on a battered pair of slippers. He loosened his collar, took off his coat and carefully hung it in a pine chifforobe. He struggled into a warm, blue robe and made his way into the kitchen. From a tall cupboard, he selected a cut glass container of bourbon and poured himself a generous drink, which he carried into the parlor. The logs in the fireplace had almost burned down to ashes, so he added two more logs and then collapsed into his favorite chair. He took an appreciative swallow of bourbon and then paused to consider what he had done.

Thirty-five years, he thought. Thirty-five years as a respected jurist and not a single blot on my record. And now? Conspiracy to obstruct justice—in a murder case, no less! Fraud? Oh, yes, definitely! And this was just the beginning. God knows where it will all end. He shook his head and took another mouthful of bourbon.

Was what he was doing worth the risk to his reputation and practice?

He had been alone now for twenty years, since his beloved Camilla had died, and they had no children. He had known and respected Champion Whittlesey from when he was a young man and admired his bride Jetta Tankard since the first day he met her. When Champion was killed in the war, Jetta had sought him out for advice, and he thought of her as the daughter he had never had.

It was all about the war, the goddam war. It had placed Jetta Whittlesey in a situation where an evil man had forced her into a mistake, a mistake for which she would pay dearly.

He was not going to let that happen, no matter what it cost him.

***

On April 10, seven days before Heartwood would be sold at public auction to pay back taxes, Jetta walked into the state of Georgia's tax assessment offices in Pembroke with a ten-thousand-dollar check in her purse. Her spirits were high, but she was outwardly calm, knowing she had a role to play in addition to satisfying the debt. "Good morning, Mr. Tift," she said brightly.

Gardner Tift, hunched over his account book, peered over his Ben Franklin glasses at his visitor. He was a small, gnome-like man, bald except for tufts of hair over his large ears and a long nose which he frequently stuck into the private concerns of his customers. His position gave him access to the most confidential financial details of the local citizenry, facts that he happily shared with anyone who asked, whether they were authorized to receive such information or not.

"Good day, Miss Jetta! What can we do for you this fine mornin'?"

Jetta delved into her purse and pulled out the cashier's check. "I am happy to pay the state what I owe in back taxes," she announced proudly.

Tift's jaw dropped. He accepted the check and asked, "Where in the world did you get the money?"

None of your business, you little snoop! "The Lord was looking out for me, surely!" she said. "An investment company in Philadelphia put a sizable amount of money in Heartwood in exchange for a mortgage on the property."

"How much they give you?" demanded Tift, practically salivating with the news.

Jetta shook her head coyly and shook her finger at the man. "Now Gardner, you know I can't give you all the details. But it's enough for me to do all the needed repairs and pay all my debts. I am truly blessed."

"That's wonderful news! I can't wait to tell all them Yankees waitin' for the sale that they ain't gonna get their hands on yer' property!"

Little man, that's exactly what I hoped you would do!

3

Chapter Three: Follow the Money

The evening after his meeting with Healy, Duckett lay in his bed in a Chicago boardinghouse staring at the ceiling and thinking about what he had learned from his friend. Certainly, Rourke was even more dangerous than his original assessment and also very smart. Anyone trying to separate Rourke from his money stood a very good chance of being killed. Except for the man in the Atlanta train station, Rourke had made a clean escape from his former life. Some would guess that he was in Georgia, but only one man knew why he was there. If Duckett was successful in convincing Rourke to pay for the privilege of keeping his privacy, he could count on Rourke's realizing that only one man knew about his interest in Heartwood plantation and the Whittlesey family, and that man was Thomas Duckett. The only way to escape Rourke's retribution if he was successful was for Duckett to change his name and where he lived and to take on a new line of work. That was possible only with money.

But suppose Rourke had been lured to leave his comfortable life by someone else who had designs on his money? Duckett remembered his prior visit to Heartwood, where he had discovered that Jetta Whittlesey, widow of Colonel Champion Whittlesey, was facing bankruptcy and the possible loss of her home. Suppose Jetta had lured Rourke to Heartwood and killed him? Certainly, a woman was less formidable a foe for him than a man.

***

The next morning Duckett put together a plan. He would take a leave of absence from Pinkerton and retrace Rourke's journey to Heartwood, if that is where he went. He had not disclosed the second five thousand dollars Rourke had paid him for his service to his company, so he could afford the trip. Based on what he learned, he would make up his mind on what to do.

***

When Thomas Duckett's train arrived at the Atlanta railroad terminal, he gathered up his coat and suitcase and made his way out of his rail car where he was greeted by two undulating streams of people either departing the trains or pushing to gain entrance to one. Porters strained to pull long wagons piled high with suitcases of every description. Men tried to maneuver their heavy bags through the thick traffic, muttering faint apologies when the bags met human contact. Ladies in smart attire walked confidently through the confusion, trailed by porters hefting multiple bags under their arms. An attractive woman in a brown travel outfit with matching hat and veil gave the neatly dressed young man an appraising glance and earned a smile and a tip of his hat. Overhead, a sea of workers moved confidently along the plank walks of a high scaffold, installing glass panels of a new roof to replace the old one burned by General Sherman's soldiers.

Duckett weaved his way through the traffic and took refuge in a small coffee shop where he bought a big mug of coffee for a nickel and carried it to a small table.

I wonder if Terrance Rourke sat here and made plans for the next move of his disappearance, he thought. What would I do if I were in his shoes? The suitcase! Filled with three million dollars! Heavy, very heavy. Dangerous thing to carry around. Needs to be stored in a safe base. A bank would be perfect. Can't use your real name, of course.

Duckett was an avid reader of Chicago newspapers, and he knew that many traditional southern banks had failed after the Civil War and were gradually being replaced by national banks formed by the National Bank Act of 1863 to create a new currency called the greenback. To discourage state banks from continuing to issue their own paper money, the federal government imposed a 10% tax on such specie. The greenback was rapidly replacing all other forms of currency in the South, but the process was slow. Rourke's supply of fresh currency would be welcome by any Atlanta bank without question.

Leaving the coffee shop, Duckett walked down the corridor until he found a place where he could check his suitcase and an information counter where he bought a small Atlanta map. From the clerk, he found the names and addresses of the three national banks in Atlanta, which he recorded in a small ledger

Leaving the depot, Duckett was startled by a loud crash and clouds of dust that caused pedestrians to have fits of coughing. The ruins of a burned building across the street were being demolished. Before the dust had settled, workmen wearing bandannas across their faces started shoveling the debris into the backs of sturdy wagons driven by mule teams. Atlanta was wasting no time regaining its title as the manufacturing and commercial center of the South. Down the street lounged a troop of Union soldiers, the last of up to nine thousand men sent by Congress to take over the state when it refused to comply with the mandate to give the Negroes their freedom and to elect new leaders who were not staunch Confederates. The citizens of Atlanta, especially the women, walked by the soldiers as if they were invisible.

After a short walk, Duckett came upon the first of the three national banks he planned to visit. The National Bank of Georgia appeared to be brand new with a few glaziers finishing the last details on its front windows. The bank was busy with people standing patiently in line to be served. Duckett informed a teller that he had urgent business with the bank manager and soon was escorted into the office of a distinguished man named Joshua Wordsworth. The manager examined Duckett's credentials, which indicated he was an investigator with the Pinkerton Detective Agency.

"So, Investigator Duckett, how can I be of service?"

"Sir, I would like you to read this article that appeared recently in a Chicago newspaper, then take a close look at the accompanying photo."

Wordsworth took the paper, then reached into a drawer for a pair of gold half-moon glasses. He studied the news article about Rourke intently, then handed it back to Duckett and removed his glasses.

"Are you here to determine if the money in question has been deposited in our bank, Mr. Duckett?"

Duckett looked pained. "No, sir, I am not. The Rourke family is convinced that he suffered some sort of mental breakdown, and they want to find him and return him to his home for care and treatment. They think the money makes him a walking target for any opportunist. Once Mr. Rourke is safe, the matter of the money will be addressed by the courts."

Wordsworth nodded and sat back in his chair.

"That certainly is a good plan. I wish I could tell you that Mr. Rourke deposited his money with us, but unfortunately, he did not. A sum so large, I would have handled it personally." The manager rose and extended his hand. "Good luck on your quest, young man!"

"Thank you, sir."

"One down, two to go," thought Duckett. He was pleased with his made-up story about Rourke's mental problems and decided to keep it in his future presentations.

The Bank of Atlanta was housed in a very prestigious building, wrought iron, marble, white stone and tall mahogany carved doors. It gave off a clear message to those who approached: To those with money who want more, welcome. To all others, you have come to the wrong place. A handsome young man in a black morning coat greeted Duckett and escorted him to the bank manager, Wilson Makepeace. He listened silently to Duckett's story, accepted and read the offered article and then looked directly at the young Pinkerton man.

"Mr. Duckett, it is the policy of the Bank of Atlanta to not divulge any information about our clients, including whether or not anyone is a customer of ours. There are no exceptions to this rule."

"Mr. Makepeace, that is surely a wise policy. I am assisting a family that suspects the father has fallen ill and is attempting to locate him before someone takes advantage of his situation. Once he is found, the authorities and courts will take over."

Makepeace stood, indicating the meeting was over. "I hope you are successful in your efforts. But we stand by our commitment never to divulge any information about our clients. Good day to you."

The bank manager's office was located in the open, toward the back of the bank, where he could view all operations. Duckett had noticed that the last teller in the line of tellers, whose position was to the rear of Makepeace's office, had seemed to be quite interested in their conversation. He was a tall, thin man with a sallow complexion, a prominent Adam's apple and neatly combed hair parted exactly in the middle. As Duckett turned to leave the bank the man offered a slight smile and a wink.

When Duckett left the bank, he consulted his timepiece and observed that it was almost noon. He crossed the street to where there was a small bar with outdoor tables and colorful umbrellas and ordered a beer. In a few minutes, the teller came striding out of the bank, looking left and right. When he saw Duckett, he carefully made his way across the busy street and entered the bar, taking a seat at an indoor booth and paying no attention to the Pinkerton man.

Duckett picked up his beer and his hat and joined him. He placed his beer on the table, rested his hat on the bench beside him and slid into the bench opposite the teller. He extended his hand across the table and introduced himself.

"Thomas Duckett, representing Pinkerton Detective Agency."

"I am Francis Cullen, Mr. Duckett, head teller for the Bank of Atlanta. I wish to apologize for the somewhat rude reception you received from our general manager."

"I am hopeful that you can remedy that situation for me, Mr. Cullen."

Cullen gave a small shrug of his shoulders. "Possibly I can, Mr. Duckett, after some negotiation, of course. May I have a look at the newspaper article you showed Mr. Makepeace?"

Duckett removed the article from his briefcase and handed it to the teller. He read the entire article and then proceeded to read it again. He refolded it neatly and handed it back to the Pinkerton man.

"I believe I can be of assistance to you Mr. Duckett. You understand that to do so, I put myself at considerable risk of being dismissed from my position if my assistance became known to my employer. Let us begin with a list of specific information that you need, and then we can discuss my fee."

Duckett gave the request some thought before answering. "I need to know if Terrance Rourke, the man pictured in the newspaper, made a visit to your bank recently and the date of that visit. If he was using a name other than his real name, I need to know what that name was and what address he gave you for future contact. I need to know specifically what services he requested from your bank and if you agreed to perform those services. If those services included depositing a sum of money, I want to know the amount of that deposit. If Rourke gave any hint of his future plans or when he might return, I want to know that as well. This information will help Mr. Rourke's family find him before he gets in trouble." He removed his breast wallet from his coat and laid it on the table. "If you can give me this information and it proves to be correct, I will give you five hundred dollars."

Cullen smiled and shook his head.

"You must excuse me, Mr. Duckett, but I have been dealing with wealthy clients for many years, and I know how they think. I do not believe you have had that experience, so naturally your plan is flawed. The newspaper article you showed me indicates Terrance Rourke devised an almost foolproof disappearance act, perfect except for a random encounter with a business acquaintance. But he left his business partner and family the bulk of his estate, so he left them in excellent condition. He took his share of the estate in cash because a draft or check would have identified him when he opened a new account. Every step he made screams a message: I am tired of my old life and have begun a new one! If that conclusion is obvious to me, it must be crystal clear to his wife. Rourke left everything but a crayon message on his shaving mirror that said, Goodbye! Do not look for me!
"

"I think you are guessing. You do not know his wife or what her reaction would be."

"Suppose you are correct and Mrs. Rourke calls for an all-out effort to find her husband. Do you think her advisors would send a young Pinkerton agent to look for him? Absolutely not! They would call on their bankers and their attorneys, and those powerful gentlemen would come to Atlanta and call on every bank in the city! And they would be cordially accepted and any information instantly shared."

"So why am I here?"

Cullen spread his arms. "You are here because of the money, Mr.

Duckett! Some of it, or perhaps all of it. My guess would be that you had some dealings with Mr. Rourke in the past, in the course of which you have some clue as to his present whereabouts. Perhaps you think that you can threaten Rourke with exposing his new life, and he will pay you to keep his secret. You have a chance to become a very rich man…"

"Or a very dead one," said Duckett.

"Precisely. But if you have a smart inside partner, your chances go up considerably."

Duckett thought for a moment and then made a decision. "What is your proposal?" he asked.

Cullen shrugged his shoulders. "I am not greedy, Mr. Duckett. I want 25% of whatever moneys you are able to recover. Since I will be aware of any withdrawals from the account, I will know exactly how much my share will be."

"We have an agreement," said Duckett and extended his hand, which the banker shook.

"Now, Mr. Duckett, I have some information for you. Do you wish to make some notes?"

The Pinkerton man removed a tablet and a pen from his briefcase. "Go ahead."

"Terrance Rourke visited our bank on the morning of April the sixth, carrying a large portmanteau. He gave his name as Parker Kellogg and said he represented a group of investors interested in real estate opportunities in Georgia and he wanted to deposit the cash in our bank."

I'll be damned! He is using the same name I used when I did my investigation for him!

Cullen cocked his head. "Good news, Mr. Duckett?"

"Yes! Please continue."

"Rourke deposited the sum of two million seven hundred and fifty thousand dollars in a savings account and the bank agreed to pay him six percent interest on the money. The cash was in greenbacks sealed by paper bands indicating it came from the First National Bank of Chicago."

So, he held out two hundred and fifty thousand that he has in his possession.

"Our bank manager pressed him for an address, but Mr. Rourke said he would be on the move, but he would arrange for a post office box in the near future where we could contact him."

Probably in Atlanta or Savannah, under his assumed name. "Did he give you any clue as to where he was going?" asked Duckett.

"No, but there is some other interesting information that you neglected to ask for, Mr. Duckett. The account is registered in the name of Parker Kellogg and/or Jetta Whittlesey of Heartwood plantation near Savannah. Is that helpful to your search, Mr. Duckett?"

"Wait! 'and/or' meaning either party has full access to the money?"

"Precisely, Mr. Duckett."

"So, Rourke and Jetta Whittlesey must have some sort of consensual relationship! I know from a prior trip that she is a widow."

"You are guessing, my friend, and that can get you into big trouble. You need to visit the plantation, preferably without being observed or identified, and determine what is happening. I will keep watch here and make my own observations. Then we will meet and make our plans. I suggest we both rent a slot in the nearest telegraph office in case something happens quickly."

Duckett frowned. "Suppose Rourke is dead and buried. How will I know that?"

The banker smiled and reached out to lay a hand on the Pinkerton man's shoulder. "If he is alive, you will see him walking around the plantation with his arm around the widow Whittlesey. If he is dead, the widow will be walking into my bank with a new dress!"

4

Chapter Four: The Night Riders

"Momma! Momma!"

Paul Whittlesey rushed into his mother's parlor like a small tornado, followed by a bemused Jubal, who crossed his arms and leaned against the door jamb. Jetta put down the lace tablecloth she was attempting to repair and gave her full attention to her five-year-old son. Paul was short and stocky, with black hair that resisted all overtures from a comb, big brown eyes that missed very little and an inexhaustible supply of energy and curiosity.

"Yes, Paul, come in, dear. What have you done to your shirt?"

The young boy regarded his shirt with surprise and tentatively touched the large red stain.

"Chokeberries?" he offered tentatively.

"Please tell me you were not eating them!"

"No, momma, I was playing war games and needed some blood!" He offered two red-stained hands in proof.

"Please go wash your hands and give Tiny your shirt before you touch anything," she scolded, trying to keep her tone stern.

The boy disappeared but quickly rushed back, his hair tentatively parted, his hands clean and wearing a fresh shirt with a minority of its buttons engaged.

"Momma! There is a full moon tonight and Jubal wants to take me and Toby coon hunting! Can I go, please?"

Jetta lifted her eyes to her Negro overseer, who nodded.

"Sleep in de wagon 'wit de dogs," he said.

"Momma, can I take father's squirrel gun? I will be really careful, I promise."

Jetta nodded. "You may take the gun if you let Jubal load it and you use the shooting stick." Paul was short and the gun was light but six feet long. A wooden branch with a "Y" at the end enabled him to aim and shoot it successfully. "And you must clean it when you return," she added.

"I promise!" he said and rushed out of the room.

***

At dusk, the small hunting party moved slowly down the old lumber trail winding through the fragrant pine trees, Hannibal, the sleek black mule, pulled the wooden wagon carrying Jubal, the two boys and the coon dogs Jess and Sissy. The dogs migrated from one side of the wagon to the other, sniffing the air for any signs of prey that would merit a chase. Jubal stopped once to check two game traps he had put out earlier that day and came back with a fat rabbit he held up by the ears. "Supper," he announced. He put his catch in a burlap bag and put it beside him on the driver's bench, safe from the two dogs.

Soon, they came to a clearing with the charred remains of many campfires. Jubal unhitched the mule and tethered him to a tree with a long rope. He sent his son, Toby, to the nearby river to fill a bucket of water and dumped some feed for Hannibal on the ground from a bag on the wagon. He removed a short axe from under the wagon seat and began cutting a small fallen tree into logs for the fire. Paul took an empty burlap bag and began filling it with fallen pinecones.

Toby returned with an armful of pine logs and assorted sticks, which he dumped near the fire site. He selected three long sticks and pruned them with the hatchet so that each ended in an open fork. Two of the sticks he chopped in half, then cut the ends to sharp points and pushed them down into the ground on either side of the fire. He walked to the wagon and came back with a thin iron bar sharpened to a point on both ends and a block of wood with a narrow hole drilled into it. He pushed one end of the rod into the wooden block until it fit tightly, then laid the rod over the two y-shaped branches. He gave the block of wood an experimental turn and was satisfied with the result, then removed the rod.

Jubal carefully skinned the rabbit, setting the remains aside for the dogs. He rubbed the carcass with a mixture of salt and herbs then skewered it with the iron rod. He made a mound of wood shavings and pinecones in the middle of the pit and built a small fire, slowly adding kindling until he had a robust blaze. When it was reduced to a bed of hot coals, he placed the skewered rabbit over the fire, and Toby began to turn it slowly. The two dogs sat near the fire with rapt attention as the smell of cooking meat rose.

When the meat was done Jubal carefully pushed it onto an old, dented pot and cut it into portions which he doled out onto pewter plates. He added some fig jam and cornbread that he had brought from home, and the trio began their meal. Paul finished his portion quickly and Jubal shared some of his meal with the boy. When everyone was finished, Toby scraped the plates and saved the scraps for the dogs. Jubal carefully loaded the game musket and slung it over his shoulder. He suddenly stood still and gazed intently to his left.

"What's the matter, Jubal?" asked Paul.

Jubal pointed a long arm. "Fire," he said. He knew they were still on Heartwood land, so there should have been no intruders. There was no storm to trigger lightning that would have caused a blaze. "Toby, put out de fire an' hitch up the mule. Tie up them dogs an' keep um quiet. I be back soon."

"Can we come along?" asked Paul. Jubal shook his head and entered the forest.

The full moon made his progress easier, and he soon had progressed to the source of the fire, a large bonfire in the middle of a clearing. He got down on all fours and crept closer, using his hand to carefully push back a thick branch on a large bush. The fire illuminated twenty hooded, white-robed figures in a half circle intently watching a shirtless young Negro man digging a narrow grave. Another hooded man stood beside the grave with an elongated crop, striking the Negro man on the back when he slowed his digging. One heavy-set Klansman sat on a stump and watched the flogging. Eventually, he stood up and called out, "That's enough!" He stepped up on the stump and turned to face his audience. "Brothers of the Klan! Almost five years ago we ended our war with the Union. We gave up our weapons and returned to our burned homes and ravaged fields. We didn't waste time but began immediately to rebuild our state. We agreed that our Negros were free men and no longer slaves, and we agreed to pay them wages when they worked in our fields.

"To our great surprise, we received help from President Johnson." The white clad riders gave a ragged cheer and called out, "Johnson! Johnson!"

"He forgave our leaders who led our cause and returned to them their property that had been seized and given to Negro people. He allowed them to take their original positions in government from which they had been banned. He ordered the Freedmen's Bureau, which had been founded to protect the Negro, to make sure that they returned to the fields or some other form of gainful work. Slowly but surely, we all began to prosper, Negroes and whites together. But our cotton profits suffered because many Negroes wanted to own and work small farms or work limited hours on the plantations.

"Our progress made the Radical Republicans in Congress very unhappy! They thought we had not suffered enough for our sins of secession. They overruled our President and sent their armies to occupy our state and to rule us by martial law, again. They removed our leaders from public office and replaced them with Yankees, carpetbaggers and scallywags! They lined their pockets with our money!"

The crowd booed loudly and brandished their rifles in the air.

The speaker held up his arms until the mob quieted. "The worse thing was to pass two amendments to our constitution that permitted the Negro to vote and to hold public office! Negro men who could barely read and write with no knowledge of our government and its function, sitting in our legislature and making laws we had to obey! And that, my friends, is when we formed the Ku Klux Klan.

"Our goal is to keep the Negro man in his place, away from the voting booth and our legislature. We began with threats and then with physical force. If those acts do not work, we will do what we shall do today, make them dig their own graves and bury them in the ground!" An appreciative roar rose from the gathered men in white.

Jubal knew the Negro man standing in the grave. Wilson Lowe was a retired sergeant in the Union Army. His service entitled him to buy one of the pieces of land on the Whittlesey plantation that had been seized by General Sherman after his successful Georgia campaign. Sherman promised "Forty acres and a Mule" to deserving Negro people. Lowe had a thriving small farm, a hard-working wife and two stalwart young boys. Recently he had been making appearances at local Negro churches to announce he was running for office in the House of Representatives.

Got yo' self in a tight! Me an' this ole squirrel gun ain't gwan save you, for sure. Maybe I try if the boys not wit' me. Too bad! Good man!

Jubal noticed some movement in the ranks of the crowd as they parted and allowed a tall man on a grey horse to come slowly forward. He wore the same Klan white robe, but his hood was red instead of white. When he turned his horse to face the crowd, Jubal noticed that the sleeve on his left arm was empty and was pinned to his side.

The tall rider stared at the assembled Klansmen for a long moment and then asked, "Who called this meeting?"

The men looked at each other until one man pushed his horse a step forward. "He did," he said, pointing to the man standing on the stump.

The man with the red headpiece slowly turned his mount and walked it over to where the big man was standing on the stump with his arms crossed. The rider pulled his white outfit back from his right side to expose a Navy Colt revolver in a holster. "You have something to say to me?" he asked the big man on the stump.

"Damn right I do!" he exploded. "Every day, the Negroes get bolder 'cause there's nobody to put them in their place! Three of them includin' him and two others, are running for office in the House of Representatives!" He gestured with his thumb at the Negro man in the trench. "We got to stop ridin' round at night with torches and start killin' niggars! And you won't do that!"

"No, and I have a good reason. There is a Negro Union regiment stationed in Savannah. They are well-trained and are battle-hardened. So far, they have not bothered us much, but when the first Negro man is killed here, they will come through our town like the wrath of God! In a week, they will have all our names and pick three of us to hang."

"You're gutless," sneered the man.

The rider put slight pressure on his mount's flanks. It surged forward and knocked the man to the ground. He struggled to his knees and tried to reach for his gun until he looked up and saw the black Colt pointed at his head. "We already got a grave dug. Seems a shame not to use it. You want to volunteer?" When his target did not respond, he said, "Put your gun on the ground. Slowly! Then walk over and join the others." When the man complied, he holstered his own weapon and swung off his horse. He walked over to the fresh grave site and motioned with his right hand for the man with the whip to join the others, then turned his attention to the Negro man standing in the grave who stared back at him without comment.

On the ground in front of the grave was a crumpled blue Union jacket. The hooded man leaned over and picked it up. He shook it and then held it up to examine the decorations and medals on the right side. He nodded and then tossed the jacket to the man in the grave, who caught it and slowly pulled it over his torso, wincing from the contact with the angry welts on his back.

"Name, rank and division?" asked the hooded man.

Something about the tone of the voice triggered an automatic response from the Negro man in the hole and he slowly came to attention. "Sergeant Wilson Lowe, sir. Fifty Fourth Massachusetts Infantry."

The hooded man nodded at the long red scar on the Negro man's abdomen. "Where did you get that souvenir, Sergeant?"

"Fort Wagner, Charleston, sir."

The hooded man shook his head. "You are damn lucky to be alive, Sergeant! What the hell is wrong with you? You survived the war. You are a free man. You have a wife, two sons and a nice farm even after we burned your corn crop. Why do you keep pushing your luck?"

"Sir, I fought for those rights as an American citizen, even shed blood for them."

"Are those rights worth dying for, Sergeant?"

The Negro man gave a small smile. "Isn't that what we soldiers do, sir?" he asked.

The masked man stared at the soldier for several seconds, then nodded. "Watch your back, Sergeant," he said as he turned to walk away. He strode confidently over to the silent circle of men in white and looked into the face of each man. "We will have a meeting next week at the usual place. At that time, we will have a vote to determine if you still want me as Grand Wizard or you want to elect someone else. I will abide by either outcome. DISMISSED!" Slowly the masked men got on their mounts and rode away.

The Grand Wizard walked over to his horse and threw the reins over its head. He grabbed the pommel with his right hand, put his left foot into the stirrup, took two short hops and gracefully swung into the saddle. The young Negro sergeant had crawled out of the grave and was watching. As the hooded man turned to leave, Lowe came to attention and saluted. The rider returned the salute and rode away.

Sergeant Lowe hurried over to the spot where the big Klansman had dropped his pistol and picked it up. He checked the number of rounds in chamber and started to stick the gun in his trousers when he heard a noise behind him. He whirled around and pointed the gun at the tall Negro man with a long squirrel gun over his shoulder. "Jesus, Jubal! I almost shot you! What are you doin' here?"

The suggestion of a smile crossed the tall Negro man's face. "Come to show you how t' kill bunch a' white trash' wit' a squirrel gun. Kin you walk?"

"Yeah' Jus' take it slow."

***

Wilson Lowe sat backward on a chair in the kitchen at Heartwood while Jetta and Tiny cleaned his back and carefully applied a healing salve. Jubal entered the kitchen and silently offered him a clean white shirt, which he carefully donned. "Feels better already," he said.

"Wilson, you must report this incident to Sheriff Barksdale," said Jetta. "And I really think you should reconsider running for office this year. It took a while for white people to accept the idea of freedom for your people, but now they have accepted that reality. The same thing will happen with Negroes running for office. Give them some time."

Lowe arose and gingerly stood upright. "Sheriff Barksdale is a good man, but he has only two deputies. I plan on going to Savannah next week and reporting what happened to the office of the Freedmen's Bureau. They have Federal troops to patrol our area and the authority to conduct an investigation to uncover the local Klan members. In the meantime, I plan to fortify my house."

"What about your idea of running for congressman?" she asked.

He shook his head. "My people are free, but our local government is still controlled by people who are set in the old ways. We need to be represented so we can argue for our rights as citizens. And that I intend to do."

***

The Fifty-Fourth Massachusetts Infantry, Wilson Lowe's old outfit, was one of the Federal units detailed to impose martial law in Georgia after the second phase of Reconstruction was enacted. Wilson sent word to Sergeant Festus Tyler, his old friend and mentor, to meet him at a riverfront bar in the Negro section of Savannah. When he spotted his younger friend, Festus grabbed him in a bear hug.

"Ow! Let up Festus!" he cried.

Five foot five inches tall with three hundred pounds of muscle, Festus frowned and asked, "What you done to yo' self now?"

They sat at a rickety table in the back of the bar, and Wilson told him about running for office and the attacks from the Klan, including the incident with the open grave.

"Sweet Jesus! Can't believe them bastards didn't kill you!" he exclaimed.

"Next time they will, no doubt 'bout it. The Grand Wizard served in the war and lost an arm, for sure. Think he looked at my scars and gave me a break."

Festus grunted and leaned back in his chair. "Lemme talk to my Colonel, see if'n we can git some patrols down your way."

Wilson was silent for a moment, then said, "What I really hope you can do is find me three more carbines so I can take care of myself."

"Who for?"

"My wife and two boys. Already taught the boys how to shoot. Simon's almost as good as me."

"I kin do that. Meet me here same time next week."

"How much I owe you?"

"Listen up, son. I didn' drag yo skinny' ass off that beach in Charleston to let some Reb kill you all over again. Them guns is on de house!"

5

Chapter Five: Into the Lion's Den

Thomas Duckett thought he had made a very successful beginning in his search for Terrance Rourke and his three million dollars. He knew exactly where the money was, at least for the present, and he had an accomplice who could help him get his hands on some or all of it. He was almost certain Rourke was at Heartwood, either alive or dead. If Rourke were alive there was a chance he would be willing to part with some of the money to guarantee his privacy, provided the blackmailer was not overly greedy. If he were dead, his killer might be willing to pay even more money to avoid arrest. In either case, it was time for Duckett to make another visit to Heartwood to see if he could determine if his quarry was on the premises or not, preferably without exposing himself.

Before he went to the train station, he visited three pawn shops in Atlanta until he found what he wanted, a military spyglass in a leather case.

"She's a beauty," said the clerk. "Most probably belonged to a Union officer. Perfect 'cept for one little nick. Five bucks, greenbacks."

"I'll take it," said Duckett.

While waiting for his train in the busy station, he gave some thought to how he could determine if Rourke was a welcome guest at Heartwood. On his previous visit, financial information on the plantation was available from local lawyers and businessmen he could call upon in his role as an agent for northern investors looking for plantation land. More specific information on the Whittlesey family was much harder to come by, although there was general agreement among the men that Jetta Whittlesey was a Southern lady of great beauty and charm who had done an excellent job in keeping her plantation operational in very difficult times. Information about Jetta's son, young Paul, had come from a young lady named Abigail Simpson, who was a friend of Jetta Whittlesey and went to the same church. Duckett had frequently visited the local barbershop and had attended the Methodist church twice. He had met Abigail during the tea party following the service. The first Sunday, he had walked her home and made plans to meet with her again the following Sunday. The third time, he had treated her to a horse and buggy ride and a picnic lunch fixed by his landlady. Unfortunately, Jetta Whittlesey had not made an appearance at either of the church services.

Abigail was a single woman with no family. She earned her way by playing the organ at church services and weddings. She had a lovely voice and a pleasing personality, but was somewhat plain in appearance. The attention she had received from Thomas Duckett had thrilled her, and when he left without saying goodbye, she had been crestfallen. She knew him as Parker Kellogg.

***

When the conductor in the Chicago station sounded the call for his train, Duckett was surprised to see it was a brand-new model, glistening on the outside with comfortable new seats that looked like they had never been used. In his march through Georgia, General Sherman's engineers had decimated the state's railroad system, not only pulling up the rails and torching the cars but heating the rails and twisting them around telegraph poles. The new Republican administration realized that replacing the rail system had to be the first step in bringing their economy back to life. Fortunately, there were plenty of Yankee businessmen who were willing to invest in such projects at a very comfortable interest rate, and there were at least six new railroads in progress.

Even the little town of Pembrook showed some improvement since his last visit. The railroad station had a new roof, the small courthouse had a new coat of paint and the single main street had repaired all its potholes. The general store was doing a brisk business.

When Duckett stepped off the train, he walked over to the stable where he had rented a horse on his last scouting visit. He found the owner chewing tobacco and leaning a chair against the stable wall.

'Mornin' Mr. Pollit. I'm back again."

"Hullo agin', young fella. You want a rig this time or jus' a horse?"

"Just a horse, please. Is Mrs. Barrow still letting rooms?"

"She sure is. Don't think she has any boarders right now. That be nine dollars for three days, greenbacks."

How in the world did these people do business during the war without Union currency? thought Duckett. He took out his wallet and counted out the bills.

"I am supposed to meet a friend of mine here who came down earlier. Older than me, heavy set, no beard. Anybody like that rent a rig from you?"

Pollit spit out a stream of tobacco. "Yeah, fella like that come around. Not very friendly, is he?"

Duckett laughed, remembering his last encounter with Rourke. "No, you sure got that right." *His guess was right! Rourke was at Heartwood!*

"Brought my rig back two days later, real early one morning. Most likely caught the early train back to Atlanta, I reckon. Never asked for no change back, neither."

Duckett was startled. Why would Rourke go back to Atlanta so soon? To get the money?

"Has he come back yet?"

"Dunno. Could be somebody else picked him up."

Duckett pondered all the different possibilities as he rode over to Mrs. Barrow's boarding house. *Had Rourke's arrival been an unwelcome surprise and he had been sent on his way by Jetta? Hard to imagine rejecting a man who was offering you a share of three million dollars. Was there a simpler explanation? Suppose the rig was returned because he no longer needed it? But why did he need it in the first place? If his visit was anticipated, why hadn't Jetta arranged to pick him up?* He needed to do some detective work and stop speculating.

As he pulled into the yard, he found his hostess out in her vegetable patch picking peas.

"Why' Mr. Kellogg! Nice to see you again. You come back to try to buy some more property?"

"Yes, ma'am," he said as he swung down off his horse. "You hear about any plantation round here that might be available? How' bout that place, Heart-something, the one the widow owned?"

"Heartwood? The place Mrs. Whittlesey owns? Afraid you are a little late on that one."

"What happened? She get married or something?"

"Jetta Whittlesey? Not likely! She is devoted to her late husband. I see her in church once in a while, still wearing black. No, the word around is that some big company in Philadelphia made a big investment in the place. Just in time, I hear it was about to be sold for taxes."

"Good for her," he said. *What the hell is going on?* He expected to hear some talk about Rourke fixing up the place as well as being seen regularly on the premises. *Who was this Philadelphia outfit?*

"Put your horse in the barn. You old room is ready and we have your favorite for dinner, fried chicken and dumplings."

***

The next morning Duckett rose early, saddled his horse and rode out to Heartwood. He guided his mount off the road and into the trees before the plantation came into view and worked his way through the brush until he was opposite the plantation. He tied the horse to a tree and found a water oak with low branches he could climb and get a clear view of his target. After he adjusted the telescope, the house jumped into view. As the sun climbed higher, he could see small groups of the freedmen attending their various chores but there was no sign of Jetta or Rourke. The mosquitoes found Duckett and made his vigil miserable, forcing him to turn up his collar and tie his handkerchief over his face. Just before he was ready to leave, Jetta herself came out on the porch and sat in a chair. She seemed to be doing some sewing on some kind of garment. Later Jubal, the big Negro overseer, joined her on the porch for just a few minutes, then left.

Come on out, Rourke. It's a beautiful day. Join the lady on the porch. But that did not happen. He sighed and after another two-hour vigil he finally climbed down from the tree, scratching his face. Somehow, he had to find a way to make a personal call on Heartwood. Rourke would certainly want to confront any male caller if he was there, and of course he would remember Duckett. That might give rise to a dangerous confrontation if Rourke was armed. *He might be killed before he made his blackmail proposal! If Jetta were alone, that would be much safer if it meant she had killed Rourke, but it also could mean she might have no problem dispatching him in the same manner! What a mess!*

***

Jubal came out on the porch and waited until Jetta looked up from the pair of Paul's pants she was mending. "Yes, Jubal?"

"Toby bin pickin' blackberries in the woods cros' de way. Saw a man up a tree spyin' on da house."

Jetta restrained herself from looking at the woods. "Is he still there?"

Jubal silently shook his head.

"We know this was bound to happen. Rourke had at least one accomplice, and he possibly figured out that Rourke came here. But there should be no way he can prove it! What we have to do is insist we never saw Rourke again after the raid five years ago."

Jubal looked at her steadily. "Plenty room under de bush."

"No! I want no more killing!"

***

Duckett spent a miserable night. Mrs. Barrow had given him some salve for his face, but it did not seem to be helping much. The next morning, he skipped his usual shave, dressed and rode his horse into town. He tied the animal up to the rail in front of the old courthouse and went inside to the office of the clerk of the court, where a small sign identified the official as Gardner Tift. He examined the cork backboard where he had seen the notice of Heartwood's tax sale on his last visit and saw that it was missing.

"Is the sale for Heartwood still on?" he asked the clerk.

The man shook his head with ill-disguised pleasure. "Nope! All paid off, I'm happy to say."

"Is there a mortgage on the property?"

"Yep. Some Philadelphia outfit called Mainline Corporation. Two hundred forty thousand dollars."

Duckett's eyes widened. *That amount was suspiciously close to the figure the Atlanta bank cashier had reported! Why was some outside company loaning Jetta money when Rourke had more than she would need? Did Rourke himself own this company and he was using it to cover his presence?*

Duckett needed to do some more digging.

He crossed the road to the train station and went into the telegraph office. After giving his message some thought, he wired a friend of his at the Pinkerton home office and asked him to run an inquiry on Mainline Corporation in Philadelphia as a personal favor.

The next morning was a Sunday, so Duckett again rose early, shaved and dressed in his best clothes, walked over to the church, entering just as the bells stopped tolling. He saw Abigail playing the organ, but she did not see him because he sat in the last row. When the service ended and people began filing out of the church, he walked up to her and called her by name. "Miss Abigail?"

"Parker! You are back! I am so glad to see you. I thought you had forgotten me."

"No chance of that. I have been unbelievably busy. My company has sent me all over the South looking for properties."

"How long are you going to be here on this visit?"

He hesitated for a moment, then said, "Probably a week or two. Depends on how my contacts pan out."

"Wonderful! Do you have time to come downstairs and join us for tea? There are some friends I want you to meet."

"Certainly," he said. *Now comes the tricky part. If Jetta Whittlesey is here, maybe I can wrangle an invitation to the plantation and check on any signs of Rourke. If Rourke is with her now, he will recognize me and know I am a threat. If he is dead but was still using the name of Parker Kellogg, the same name I am using, Jetta will know something is wrong, and so will Abigail.*

They entered the church annex and joined the crowd, helping themselves to the tea and pastries served by the women of the church.

Abigail stood on tiptoe and looked over the crowd. "Look! There's my friend Jetta and her friend Judge Huckabee. Come and let me introduce you!"

As they made their way through the crowd, Duckett put a confident smile on his face. Huckabee, yes, I met him when I was trying to get some information on Heartwood on my first visit. But Jetta Whittlesey was a surprise: tall, striking in appearance, black hair, dark eyes. Simple, long black dress, matching shawl. Small wonder Rourke was obsessed with this woman. Any man would be attracted to her.

Jetta saw her friend Abigail weaving through the crowd, a happy smile on her face, towing a handsome young man behind her. Obviously, this was the man Abigail had met over a month ago, someone buying property for a Chicago bank. When he did not follow up on his first visit, her friend was crushed. Why did he come back? Every morning when she awoke, Jetta reminded herself that it was highly possible Rourke had used an accomplice to check up on her rather than to make the trip himself. The judge had warned her to be careful with any stranger who was possibly trying to locate Rourke. Is this the man?

"Jetta, this is my friend Parker Kellogg I have been telling you about. Parker, this is Jetta Whittlesey and Judge Abner Huckabee."

"A pleasure to meet you, Mrs. Whittlesey. Hello, again Judge. You were of great help to me on my last visit."

The judge gave a slight frown, then nodded and extended his hand. "Yes, I remember you, young man. You asked about plantations that were possibly up for sale, including Heartwood."

Parker Kellogg! That was the same name Rourke used when he wrote her a letter asking if he could visit Heartwood to make her a business proposition! He knew well that I would never allow him to set foot on the plantation if he used his real name. This young man must be the spy Rourke hired to learn about my financial problems. Odd that Rourke would make such a simple mistake as to use the same name himself.

Duckett felt Jetta's dark eyes bore into his as she extended her hand. "Welcome, Mr. Kellogg. Abigail has been telling us nice things about you."

Duckett shook her hand and said, "Mrs. Whittlesey, I had hoped that when we met, we could discuss the possible purchase of your plantation, but the treasurer's office tells me I am too late."

Jetta gave a little smile and said, "Obviously, you have met our town crier, Mr. Tift."

"I am disappointed on two points. I think my people would have paid top dollar for Heartwood, and that would have meant a healthy commission for me." Abigail frowned at his obvious social gaffe, but Jetta took no offense at his behavior.

Ah, you are slick, young man! Do you want to peer into my closets and see if you can find the missing Terrance Rourke? "That can certainly still be arranged, Mr. Kellogg. Would you and Abigail be my guests for dinner tomorrow evening? Say, around five o'clock? And Judge, would you care to join us?"

Duckett beamed. "That would be wonderful!"

When the couple left, the judge frowned. "My dear, you are inviting the fox into the hen house."

"He is going to find some way to get access to Heartwood. I prefer him to do so when I am in control of the situation instead of some midnight raid."

***

That evening, when Duckett sat on his bed and pulled off his shoes, he thought about his first meeting with Jetta Whittlesey. *A very poised, stunning woman and certainly one that Terrance Rourke would love to possess. Hell, any man would! On the other hand, it was very difficult to see her have any kind of relationship with a coarse man like Rourke. Could he see Jetta as a possible murderess?* He detected a certain layer of steel beneath all the silk.

She certainly had no hesitation in inviting him and Abigail to Heartwood for dinner, almost as if she had anticipated the request. *You don't fool me, young man! I know who you are looking for and you will not find him!* Still, he had to take a look. Maybe he would get lucky.

6

Chapter Six: The Complete Tour

Duckett rode over to the rental stable and hired a buggy to carry Abigail to the dinner at Heartwood. She emerged from her small house wearing what was obviously a handmade yellow dress, nicely accented with a fine lace collar and a wide-brimmed straw hat.

"My, don't you look nice," he said as he helped her onto the seat.

She blushed as she repositioned her hat. "Do you really like it? It just seemed like the perfect day for a bright outfit!"

It was, indeed, a perfect day. The late afternoon sun still warmed the newly plowed fields and the Negro workers as well. Many looked up from their work to wave to the young couple in the buggy. A few lonely spring flowers grew along the road, and birds celebrated the warm weather with happy songs.

"There don't seem to be many workers in the fields," observed Duckett.

"Jetta says they work only part days now, and the women stay home with their children. Once they have worked enough to earn what little they need, they go home to work in their own gardens or to hunt and fish."

"Can't she hire replacement workers?"

"She says few are available. The railroads are paying more money for workers to rebuild the tracks that Sherman destroyed during the war. And recruiters from as far away as Texas are trying to hire people to work their fields and do construction work."

When they reached Heartwood, Abigail said, "Look! The place is getting a new roof! And a new coat of paint, too." Workers were climbing down from the roof, where about a third had been replaced with bright new shingles. Painters were still working on the upstairs porch. A group of men with shovels and machetes was cleaning out the nearby ditches.

Well, she sure didn't waste any time to start spending the money, wherever it came from, thought Duckett.

Jubal came out of the house to tend to the rig, giving the Pinkerton man a long, hard stare and Jetta, herself, came out on the porch to greet them. "Abigail, what a lovely dress! And welcome to Heartwood, Mr. Kellogg."

"This place will be magnificent when you finish," said Duckett.

"We soon will be concentrating on changes to our farming operation. We are going to begin depending more on livestock and grain crops. I am giving up on cotton. It is too difficult to raise with limited labor, and you have two bad years for every good one. It is a heartbreaker."

"Do your neighbors agree with you?" asked Duckett.

Jetta gave a short laugh. "They still think cotton is king. But it was slavery that made cotton profitable. I think they will soon learn that lesson."

When they entered the foyer, Duckett was impressed. A curved stairway made its way up to the second floor on the right side, and on the left, twin doors opened to a room with a fireplace over which hung a handsome portrait of a younger Jetta Whittlesey. In the center of the back wall of the foyer was a recessed cupboard with a carved shell interior. Queen Anne chairs stood on either side. A large brass chandelier hung from the ceiling.

"What a lovely entrance," said Duckett. He felt a certain uneven feeling under his foot and looked down to see an ugly, black burned area in the wide plank pine floor.

"A little gift from General Sherman," explained Jetta. "Fortunately, the raiding party was interrupted by a unit of Confederate cavalry."

A raiding party? That was what Rourke did in the war! Was that his connection to Heartwood and Jetta? How could she have a relationship with a man who tried to burn down her home?

The party drifted into the front parlor, where Judge Huckabee was already ensconced in one of the twin loveseats in front of a waning fire and drinking a glass of sherry. Everyone sat down in front of the fire and Tiny, the Negro maid, offered them a glass of sherry from a silver tray.

"This is the most beautiful house I have ever seen," said Duckett, as he accepted a glass of sherry. "When was it built?"

"Heartwood was built in 1815 by Fulton Whittlesey, my late husband's father," said Jetta.

"I understand you lost your husband in the war. I am so sorry," said Duckett.

Jetta looked down at her hands. "Champion was a combat engineer. He had built a bridge out of old rice boats to allow the soldiers trapped in Savannah to escape to the mainland. He was attempting to set off an explosion to prevent the pursuing Union forces from attacking when the charge exploded prematurely."

She looked up and gave a brave smile. "We were lucky. When his body was recovered, he was recognized by some of the officers who had served with him in the Mexican War. One of them had actually been our guest here at Heartwood. He got permission to bring Champion's body home with an honor guard. He is buried back in the pine grove with his mother and father. I visit him every day."

At that moment, Paul Whittlesey made his entrance, freshly scrubbed, with his hair plastered down.

"Come in, Paul. Meet our guest, Mr. Kellogg." Duckett stood, and Paul approached tentatively. He looked up into the face of the tall man standing before him and asked, "Are you a Yankee spy, too?" The group exploded with laughter, which fortunately gave Jetta a chance to improvise her response. She had seen the slight frown cross Duckett's face before he laughed with the others.

"Mr. Kellogg, Paul wants to be a soldier like his father. You are only the second Yankee he has ever met. Last week an appraiser of the property visited us from Philadelphia, and Paul captured him with a wooden gun. But after the man let Paul drive his buggy, they became good friends.

Fortunately, Tiny arrived to announce dinner was served.

Jetta had arranged for Duckett to sit on her right. She knew he would try to elicit as much information from her as possible, and she did not want him to think she was ignoring him.

Tiny served a simple meal consisting of sliced ham, field greens and potatoes and passed a loaf of freshly baked bread. The meal was served on fine china plates, but the silver was mismatched and bore the sign of extensive wear. "You must excuse the condition of my silverware," said Jetta. "General Sherman's bummers found the silver my husband bought for me irresistible, along with my personal jewelry."

"I find it strange that the officer in charge of the raiders would permit that to happen," offered Duckett. "Surely it would have a terrible effect on the discipline of the soldiers involved."

"I doubt the officer in charge, a Colonel Hitchens, knew anything about the theft," said Jetta. "Just before his men executed the raid, he was injured by a bomb planted in the road by Confederate cavalry. He sustained a severe cut to his face, and one of his sergeants was killed. He was in a rage, naturally. He rode from one end of the plantation to the other, ordering the burning of our cotton crop, rounding up all livestock, killing the fowl, seizing our food supply and our cattle feed. He then rode off to raid another plantation, leaving his bummers to lay waste to the plantation. The soldiers who stripped the house found the food cellar and the valuables I had buried there, thinking it was the last place they would look. I was wrong."

"What a terrible experience," said Duckett.

"Enough talk of war. Tell me about yourself, Mr. Kellogg. How long have you been in the property business?"

"About two years, now. It is more difficult than I imagined. I thought most plantation owners would be happy to sell, but they all think a recovery in cotton is just around the corner."

"In what areas have you been prospecting?"

Duckett hesitated, then offered, "The Sea Islands, lately, since they offer both rice crops and long staple cotton."

"What are you offering per acre, if I may ask?"

"Well, it varies, but generally about ten dollars an acre."

Jetta nodded and sipped from her wine glass. *You'd best brush up on your profession, Mr. Duckett. Ten dollars an acre will buy the entire island of St. Simons, where there are two bankrupt properties begging for a buyer. And the planters there have given up on rice.*

"Tell me, Mr. Kellogg, what did you do before you chose the real estate business?"

Duckett looked directly into her eyes. "I was a detective in Chicago."

"Jetta arched her eyebrows. "Really? How fascinating! Well, if you ever tire of the real estate business, you can always go back to police work."

He smiled and took a sip of wine. "That is exactly what I plan to do."

Jetta put her napkin down and said, "I hate to interrupt, but it is growing late and I have promised a tour of the house and the garden if we have time. We can have coffee in the parlor later." Duckett stayed with Jetta and the judge took the arm of Abigail.

Jetta led the way into a large room where Tiny and an older Negro woman were washing the plates and silverware and storing them in cabinets on the walls. There was a long table where those Negroes who worked in the house could have their meals. A trio of three large windows allowed plenty of light and looked out over the garden. "The kitchen is in that separate building out there on the left, of course," said Jetta.

"Oh, my! Look at your garden!" gushed Abigail. "It is starting to bloom already!"

"I feel guilty every time I look at it," said Jetta." I have been so busy that I have neglected it. Shall we go upstairs?"

As they climbed the stairs, Duckett said, "This stairwell is magnificent! It seems to flow upstairs without any visible support, like it is floating on air."

"The original stairway was very simple. My husband Champion saw this one in a house in Atlanta and came right back home and designed this copy. He also supervised the construction."

"He must have been a very talented man," said Duckett.

"Champion was an engineer. He said one of the things he hated about war was how it destroyed so many beautiful things made by men with talent."

At the top of the stairs, she opened a door on the right, saying, "This is the master bedroom, with doors out to the upper deck." The room had a large tester bed with a white lace canopy stretched over the tall carved bed posts and a handsome oriental rug on the floor. Duckett noticed a picture of an officer in a Confederate uniform on the mirrored dressing table.

"Is that your husband?" he asked.

"Yes," said Jetta. Her voiced softened. "His photo is the first thing I see every morning and the last thing I see at night."

She led the way out of the room and crossed the hall to the next room. "This is the main guest room, and we have another in the back of the house." Like the master bedroom, it had a wide fireplace with two comfortable chairs and two matching beds separated by a table. French doors led out to the porch. Duckett took a quick look and then stood aside so Abigail could see. Suddenly, he had a sense of encountering something important, something he could not define. In an instant the feeling passed, leaving him confused and uncertain about what he was experiencing.

Jetta pointed to another room with a closed door and said, "I think we will skip Paul's room. He did not inherit Champion's neatness!" She led the group back down the curved stairway, through the hall and out the door to the back porch. The sun had begun to set, its diminished rays giving a final embrace to the three terraces of Jetta's extended garden. The first tier was an herb garden of culinary and medical plants including thyme, rosemary, dill, marjoram and tansy. Groupings of roses and other floral plants were interspersed with the herbs.

"What is that beautiful bush with the blood-red flowers?" asked Duckett.

Jetta looked at him strangely and then answered, "That is a quince bush, a gift from my husband on the day he went to war. Be careful if you approach it! It has very sharp thorns."

The area was bisected by a brick walk leading to a pergola and stairs leading down to the second level that featured espaliered fruit and an expansive vegetable garden where three Negroes were working with hoes. Another set of steps led down to the final tier, where there was a large barn and the ruins of two other burned buildings. A wide river lapped at the boundary of the property.

"The raiders burned the cotton gin and a building where we kept most of the tools and seeds," said Jetta. "They took all our horses and most of our mules. They took my favorite grey mare, Duchess, that I had raised from birth. I still hate them for that." She led the party down a path to the right that ended in a grove of pine trees.

"This is the resting place of all the members of the Whittlesey family, including my husband, Champion." She walked over to a tall simple stone with the inscription

CHAMPION S. WHITTLESEY
1825-1864

A single red rose lay at the base of the stone. Jetta turned to Duckett and said, "I come here the first thing every morning to relive all the good times and try to forget the pain. Sometimes it works."

"What is the symbol carved on the headstone?" asked Duckett.

"That is the Confederate Medal of Honor, awarded by Jefferson Davis himself."

***

After he had taken Abigail home, Duckett returned to the boarding house, kicked off his shoes and collapsed on his bed. His mind was a confusion of impressions, facts and new questions. *Jetta Whittlesey was a lovely, intelligent woman who obviously moved easily in the top strata of Georgia aristocracy. She had loved and admired her late husband and missed his presence after he had died so tragically. What attraction would such a woman have for a man like Terrance Rourke, a rough and crude bully who, five years ago, had been a sergeant in Sherman's forces that had possibly ravaged her plantation? Yes, he had money, but money would not bridge such a cultural difference. On the other hand, Rourke was smart too. It seemed unlikely he would have given up his successful life in Chicago unless he had some reason for believing Jetta would entertain his advances. He had made her a co-owner of his bank account in Atlanta! Why would he do that without some assurance that his overtures would be accepted?*

If I could find him, I could ask him, he thought. Obviously, he is not at Heartwood. He would be on the porch with his cigar and his arm around Jetta! Did he make his generous offer, and she refused it? If so, where was he now? There must be other beautiful widows in Georgia, and Atlanta would be a perfect city for a man like Rourke.

Duckett had been reading Mrs. Barlowe's newspapers and they were full of criticism of Georgia's governor, a one-time Radical Republican Yankee named Bullock who had taken advantage of all the state building and railroad projects to cut himself a healthy portion of the graft usually evidenced in those projects. Rourke could double his fortune in no time in such an environment.

Was it possible for a woman like Jetta Whittlesey to kill Terrance Rourke? She would not have to do the deed herself; that big Negro overseer looked capable of killing anyone at her request. But what would be the motive? Did Rourke tell her about the money in their joint names waiting in the Atlanta bank, and she decided to claim it all for herself? She would have to make the journey to Atlanta with proof of her identity, and the bank would certainly want consent from Rourke himself, or at least a death certificate. Duckett had made arrangements with his fellow conspirator at the bank to telegraph him if there was any news about movement of the money, and so far, there was no such contact. He shook his head in frustration. *Maybe a good night's sleep would help.*

The next morning Duckett woke to the tantalizing smell of fresh-baked bread. He threw back the covers and stretched, then suddenly realized what had bothered him back in Jetta's guest bedroom: the cloying smell of a man's cologne called Lilac Vegetal! He was familiar with the scent because an old girlfriend of his back in Chicago had given him a bottle for Christmas. He had tried it only once and had to wash it off. When his client in Chicago had interviewed him from behind a partition, Duckett had been aware of two smells: a good Cuban cigar and that familiar cologne.

Rourke had spent some time in Jetta's guest bedroom! And that fact gave rise to another mystery: If he and Jetta had some sort of relationship, why was Rourke sleeping alone?

7

Chapter Seven: The Political Education of Sergeant Lowe

Joseph Feeney, more commonly known as "Knuckles" Feeney, got his political education in New York politics as a ward boss for William Tweed, aka Boss Tweed, who controlled the Irish-Italian area known as Tammany Hall. Feeney was a big man, six foot three, with wide shoulders, quick hands and a deceptively jovial disposition. It was his job to make sure that the local Democratic party under Tweed maintained its iron grip on Tammany's politics by an effective combination of Irish charm, healthy bribes and the effective use of the brass knuckles he kept in his pocket. Feeney saw no inconsistency in beating a political opponent to within an inch of his life on Saturday and piously receiving the host at Saint Patrick's church on Sunday morning. Joe Feeney was well paid for his work. He had his pick of the liberated young women in his neighborhood, a comfortable apartment, and no bartender dared to present him a bill for the Tullamore Irish Dew that he favored in any of the neighborhood bars.

But Feeney was also a smart man, smart enough to see that a new reform movement, pushed by the city newspapers, was threatening the comfortable empire over which Tweed reigned. He had an old friend who lived in Atlanta and was keeping him posted on the political situation in Georgia under the provisional governor, Radical Republican Rufus Bullock. Taking advantage of the withdrawal of Georgia conservative Republicans and Democrats protesting the right of Negroes to vote and hold office, Bullock had packed the legislature with a loyal grouping of Negroes, carpetbaggers and sycophants. At the advice of his close friend and financial advisor, H.I. Kimball, Bullock pushed Georgia into a massive program of repairing and extending the state's railroad system, including some lines owned by Kimball himself. The ambitious program was funded by Georgia state bonds under the direction of Kimball with little oversight by the legislature.

"Everybody is on the take," advised his friend. "Construction people, railroad people, the politicians—everybody got their hand out, including the governor himself. You need to get your ass down here and get some of the action." Feeney took his advice and on January 2nd found himself in the Atlanta office of Wilbur Potts, Governor Bullock's chief of staff. Potts was a small, plump man with shifty eyes, grey hair parted neatly in the middle and the florid face of a heavy drinker. He leaned back in his chair and carefully read Feeney's summary of his varied political skills. When he was finished, he sat up straight in his chair and dropped the resume on his desk.

"Yes, you look like a man we can use," he said. "We got an election coming up in six months and your job is going to be to run herd on the Negro candidates, especially those in the cotton belt near the coast. We want to make sure we have candidates who are smart enough to sit in the legislature but who do what we tell them to do. Also, you need to monitor the registration and make sure we get a heavy Negro turnout."

"You expect any problem with the registration?" asked Feeney.

Potts shook his head. "I don't think so. Georgia is still under martial law. We have the Freedmen's Bureau and federal troops who can police the registration sites, so the Negroes don't feel intimidated. We're getting some reports of Klan activity in some counties, like Chatham, and that might be a problem. If it looks like the turnout might be a little light, there is a big group of rough Negroes who crossed over to the Sea Islands from Carolina. Get me a bunch of names and fake addresses and get them registered. Give the head man two hundred bucks and his men two dollars a head and a train ticket, and that should do it."

Feeney had been making notes in a small tablet he carried. He thought for a moment and then said, "If I was running the local Klan, I'd concentrate on the Negroes who are running for office. Makes the job a lot easier. Maybe we should hire a few tough bodyguards to watch over them."

"No, I don't want to do that. We still need some votes from the Democrats and that would make us look like we are going out of our way to take care of the Negro candidates. They have to learn to take care of themselves." He stood and went over to a small green safe sitting in the corner, fiddled with the combination and swung it open. He reached in and took out two thick wads of cash that he handed to Feeney. "Here's your first month's pay. You need any more for any reason, let me know." He reached into his vest pocket and withdrew a gold watch. "Let's get some lunch. Got three Negro candidates from Chatham County coming in for interviews."

***

Feeney and Potts sat on one side of a long rectangular table and the three Negro candidates sat on the other side. Potts had provided Feeney with resumes the men had filled in before the meeting. The Reverend Buford King was a Baptist minister in his early sixties, tall and thin with a lined face and grey curly hair and a confident bearing. He preached in three Negro churches in Chatham County and was well respected by his congregations. Roscoe Japes was a small, shifty-eyed man with a permanent frown on his face. He owned two Negro speakeasies and his breath suggested he had been sampling some of his inventory before the meeting. Wilson Lowe was a former sergeant in the Union army who had bought his small farm on the local Heartwood plantation under an offering promoted by the Freedmen's Bureau. He was married and had two sons. Something about him impressed Feeney. Slender and composed, he exuded a confidence that was evident as well as a quiet intelligence. On his resume, Feeney noted that Potts had written a note that Lowe had been threatened by the Klan, including having to dig his own mock grave. Brave man, he thought.

Potts rose to his feet and began the meeting. "Gentlemen, thank you for stepping forward to run as candidates to the Georgia General Assembly this coming June. Two years ago, in 1868, all seven candidates elected in Chatham County were white Democrats. This year we have to change that situation if we want to continue Governor Bullock's determination to enforce the rights of Negro people under the new 14th and 15th Amendments." He put his hands in his pockets and began to pace in front of the table. "We have heard rumors of new Klan activity in this area, and some of you have been the target of threats and physical abuse. If this continues, contact Mr. Feeney here for assistance. What he can't handle personally, he will call on the Freedmen's Bureau and federal troops to handle. He will also be your contact person for funds you might need to run your campaign. Suitable clothes. Entertainment. Newspaper ads. It all adds up. Anybody have any questions?"

Reverend King slowly raised his hand. He held up a folded newspaper and said, "I have been reading disturbing reports about a committee in the legislature that is investigating Governor Bullock on charges of corruption. My people greatly appreciate his efforts on our behalf, but he cannot continue to help us if he is removed from office."

Potts shook his head. "That investigation is going nowhere! We have four members on that committee, and they tell me there is not a shred of evidence for such charges. They indicate that the governor will be totally exonerated. Any other questions?"

Sergeant Lowe raised his hand. "I rode on the new Western and Albany railroad to get to this meeting and bought my own ticket. But I noticed that most riders paid no money because they had some sort of free pass. I picked one up off the floor of the station." He reached in his pocket and withdrew a small white card. "It says,' Free Pass, W & A Railroad, Courtesy of H.I. Kimball.' How will Mr. Kimball pay for his railroad if he doesn't charge for tickets?"

Potts snorted. "Don't you worry about Mr. Kimball! He has plenty of money. Matter of fact, he has a large interest in the bank used by the state of Georgia. And free tickets are a good way to get people used to riding on his train. Any more questions?"

Roscoe King raised a tentative hand. "When can we start getting the money?"

"Your candidacy has to be approved by the Republican State Committee," said Potts. "Feeney will advise you when you have been accepted. Thank you for your time, gentlemen."

***

After the candidates had departed, Potts sat at the table and cocked his eyes at Feeney. "So, Irish, what do you think of our candidates?"

"I wouldn't vote for Japes for dogcatcher; he has the look of a hard boozer. The reverend and the sergeant look really sharp—maybe too sharp. I find men of high character are hard to control."

Potts shrugged. "Where else are they going to go? For them, we are the only game in town."

***

A week later, Feeney met with the reverend and Lowe in the same office. He rose to his feet and shook hands with both men. "Congratulations, gentlemen! You both have been approved as candidates for the House of Representatives by our advisory committee. I think you both will be outstanding candidates." He sat down in his chair and folded his hands behind his head. "Since you are both new to politics, I want to give you some advice about what to expect. First, Reverend, what do you think is the most important goal of the Republican Party of Georgia?"

The Reverend folded his arms and thought for a moment. "Managing the state for the benefit of all its citizens."

Feeney turned to Wilson Lowe. "Sergeant?"

"I agree, but I would say for the benefit of all citizens of the United States."

"Good answers. Unfortunately, they are both wrong. The first goal of the party is to stay in power. If what the people need is something that also benefits the party, it will get done. If it is difficult, expensive or controversial it won't. As simple as that. If you are introducing a bill, be sure to include information on how it benefits not only the people of Georgia but also the Republican Party."

He got up and leaned on the back of his chair. "Let's talk about loyalty. The party is a very jealous mistress. You are going to find yourself in situations where the oath you take when you are elected seems to conflict with your loyalty to the party. If the issue is really important to you, vote your conscience. But don't get the reputation of being too damned independent or you will find yourself cut out of the action and stuck on some boring committee.

"I am sure you wonder how you will be treated by your fellow delegates. You will find the same kinds of people in the legislature that you find in life, from those who are friendly to those who ignore you completely. In your first year, you can win their respect by only raising your hand to speak when you have something important to say and then sitting down. Take note of the men who are courteous to you from both parties, and if you have a question, ask them for help."

"Tell us about the graft," said Lowe.

"I would be surprised if you were not propositioned on your first day, either by another congressman or one of the hangers-on. The higher up you climb, the bigger the temptation. The easiest thing to do is to refuse any gift, from a bottle of whiskey to a bag of money."

Lowe persisted. "If we find out about the crime, do we report it?"

"If what's happening is serious, it should be shared with the leaders of the party. Your problem is when the leaders are the ones doing the graft. Then you should talk to other congressmen whom you trust and let them make the moves. In the long run, if nobody acts, the public finds out, and usually the party is kicked out of office along with the thief."

"Are you on the take yourself?"

Feeney threw back his head and guffawed. "Not yet, but I just got here!"

8

Chapter Eight: Fish or Cut Bait?

Nursing a lukewarm cup of coffee, Thomas Duckett sat alone in the same small café where he had first met with Frances Cullen, the head teller of the Bank of Atlanta where Rourke had stashed the bulk of his money. But Duckett had none of the excitement and optimism he had felt on his first visit. Despite the fact that he had uncovered several clues that suggested Rourke had made an appearance at Heartwood, he had no tangible evidence of such a visit. Even more troubling was the impression that Jetta Whittlesey had made upon him. Duckett saw absolutely no way an elegant lady like Jetta would have countenanced any relationship with a rough customer like Terrance Rourke. Even if she had killed Rourke for his money or had him killed, why had she not presented herself to the bank and demanded what was legally hers? Unable to unravel the mystery, Duckett had decided to make a trip to Atlanta to consult with his new accomplice.

The bell over the entrance door tinkled as Cullen made his entrance, smiling at the lone waitress and touching the brim of his hat. He sat across the table from Duckett and carefully placed his hat on the adjoining chair. He carefully studied Duckett's face and then remarked, "Thomas, it appears that we have a problem. Bring me up to date on your efforts."

Duckett relayed how the owner of the only stable in town identified Rourke by the picture in the Chicago paper, how young Paul had asked him if he was "another Yankee," and how he had identified the faint remnants of Rourke's cologne in one of the guest bedrooms. "But what has completely eluded me is understanding any kind of relationship between Rourke and Jetta. They are two completely different people."

"Hmm." Cullen folded his arms and closed his eyes. He then leaned on the table and said, "Go over the question you asked Jetta about why Sherman's bummers didn't burn down the plantation."

"As I remember, Jetta said that a sergeant in the raiding party was killed by a road torpedo set by General Wheeler's cavalry, and the command major himself suffered a facial wound. He was furious and ordered that the plantation be stripped of foodstuffs and the house then set afire. She said that Confederate cavalry under Wheeler arrived on the scene, and the raiders did not have time to finish burning the house. There's still a large burn on the floor of the foyer you can feel with your foot."

Cullen shook his head. "That is not how the bummers generally operated. Did you know I served in the Confederate army? Never fired a shot in anger. I was in the quartermaster corps. Still, I learned a lot about war, more than I wanted to know." He leaned on the small table with both arms and rested his face in his hands.

"Sherman had two armies of thirty thousand men, and Wheeler had only ten thousand cavalrymen. Wheeler had to confine his efforts to attacks on Sherman's rear echelon and flanks, hit and run operations to slow down Sherman's columns. But Sherman's bummers were sent out in advance of Sherman's forces, close enough that they would be protected by the bulk of his army if attacked.

"The single burn on the floor in the foyer also puzzles me. The bummers had burning a plantation down to a science. A squad of men entered the house with burning pine faggots. First, half of them went upstairs and set fire to anything combustible. They rushed down the stairs, and the rest of the squad torched the downstairs. Whole operation took only minutes."

"So, what do you think happened?" asked Duckett.

Cullen held up his hand. "Patience. I want more information. I want you to tell me everything you can remember about your two conversations with Rourke when he hired you to spy on Heartwood. Leave nothing out! I want every word!"

Duckett tried to reconstruct both meetings with Rourke while Cullen listened patiently. When Duckett finished, Cullen nodded and asked, "From your account, it sounds as if Rourke was first interested in the state of the plantation and the family finances, but in the second session, he was interested in the individual family members more than their finances."

"Yes, I think that was the case."

"Which family member did Rourke ask about first?"

Duckett thought a moment and then said, "He asked if Mrs. Whittlesey was still a married woman, and I told him that she was a widow, that her husband had died a hero's death trying to blow up a bridge in Savannah while the garrison there escaped."

"And what was his response to that report?"

Duckett grimaced and said, "He posed a rather snide question about whether her husband had been 'careless with explosives,' as I remember."

"Interesting," said Cullen. "Now tell me his reaction when he found out that Jetta had a son named Paul."

"Rourke hides his feelings well, but I could tell he was very interested in the boy, how old he was, what he was like and so forth. When I told him some of Paul's antics, he laughed out loud. First time I ever heard him laugh."

"Very interesting," said Cullen. He looked into space while drumming his fingers on the tabletop. Finally, he sat up straight in his chair and looked at his fellow conspirator for a long moment. "So, our main issue is to discover what hold Rourke had on Jetta Whittlesey. I believe I have figured out the answer to that question with a fair amount of certainty, enough to allow you to approach her with a demand for money. I am happy to give you that information, but you must agree that our roles in this matter have now changed considerably."

Duckett frowned. "Changed how?"

"Up to now, you have been the dominant player in this drama and I have only played a minor role of keeping track of the money. But now you are stymied and without my plan, your scheme has come to an end. If my information is so important, I want a larger percentage of the money."

"Duckett grimaced. "How much do you want?"

"Half," said Cullen confidently.

"Absolutely not! I'm taking all the risk here if there is any retaliation! I will give you 30 percent."

"Forty percent or I am leaving."

Duckett shook his head. "Too much!"

Cullen stood, picked up his hat and carefully put it on his head. "A pleasure meeting you, Thomas. I hope you are successful in your efforts. If you are not, you know where to reach me." He turned and made his way to the door.

Duckett let him grasp the doorknob before he said, "Wait!"

Cullen swung the door half open before he paused and looked over his shoulder.

"Come back," said Duckett.

Cullen walked back to the table but did not sit down. He extended his hand and asked, "Forty percent?"

"Forty percent," said Duckett.

Cullen removed his hat and reclaimed his seat. He leaned forward on his elbows and asked, "What does Jetta Whittlesey value more than anything else in the world, more than even her own life? The answer is her son, Paul. And how can Terrance Rourke threaten Paul Whittlesey? By claiming to be Paul's father and knowing Jetta has good reason to know it's true."

"Impossible!" snorted Duckett.

"Hear me out, please. The Union major in charge of the raid on Heartwood ordered the place burned to the ground. Typically, this is done by the ranking non-commissioned officer after the plantation is thoroughly sacked. Now, it is probable that the officer in charge had command of more than one group of bummers, so after giving his orders, he probably left Heartwood. After his men had finished grabbing all the food and animals, Rourke probably put pressure on Jetta to disclose where she had hidden her valuables, which happened frequently. Maybe she resisted. He lit a torch and dragged her into the house, where he told her that if she submitted to his advances, he wouldn't burn the house down. She hesitated, he dropped the torch, she changed her mind, and the fire was stomped out.

"Now Fate played a role. Rourke ended up in Savannah where Champion Whittlesey helped the defenders escape the city by an amazing act of heroism. It is almost certain that Rourke heard of the incident. He knew Jetta was now a widow, but at first, he did nothing. Time and his financial success changed that.

"Five years later, you informed him that Jetta has a son named Paul who is five years old. A quick glance at his calendar and he knew that he was the probable father. A son, just what he always wanted, after he had fathered three girls in a row! And what a deal he offered Jetta—-he would pay off all debts, bring Heartwood back to its former glory and offer Paul any future he wishes. He was convinced no woman could resist such an arrangement." Cullen shook his head. "But one woman did. Decisively."

"So, how do we execute our plan without my suffering the same fate as Rourke?" asked Duckett.

"First, let's make a few assumptions. Let's assume Rourke is dead and was killed by Jetta's overseer. Rourke was not killed because he was a threat to Jetta. She could have summoned the sheriff and had him thrown off the plantation any time she wanted! He was killed because he wanted to raise Paul in his own image.

"I think that after Rourke's death, Jetta found the $250,000 dollars in his effects, and that was an unexpected surprise. She may have hesitated about keeping the money, but in the end, she used it to save Heartwood from foreclosure, which was about to happen."

"You don't think Rourke would have boasted about his plans to share the rest of the money with her?" asked Duckett.

"Maybe he did, but didn't tell her where it is. Maybe he did, but she doesn't want to claim it because that would be proof that she murdered him, and she wants to let sleeping dogs lie. Maybe he didn't tell her at all. Lots of maybes," replied Cullen.

"How do we get Jetta to step forward and claim the money and then share it with us?" Duckett asked.

"You have to tell her the truth and make her believe you. You have to convince her you want one million dollars, and she will never see you again! You have to point out what she could do for her son and for Heartwood if she had another $1,750,000," explained Cullen.

"And if she refuses or threatens me?" wondered Duckett.

"You already told her you have an accomplice, so she gains nothing by killing you. You can threaten to report your findings to Pinkerton, and you might get a few thousand dollars as an award and Jetta ends up in jail—not a very favorable outcome for any of us." He gazed up at the ceiling a few minutes, then looked directly at Duckett and said, "The most effective threat you can give is to tell Jetta you will spread the word that Rourke raped her and that Paul is his illegitimate son."

Cullen's directness shocked Duckett.

"Jesus!" exclaimed Duckett.

"You are about to become a criminal, Thomas. That's what you must do if you want the money. You may console yourself by reminding Jetta she gets much more money than we do or by thinking about how you will spend Rourke's greenbacks." He reached over the table and patted his partner on the shoulder. "Tell me when you make up your mind."

After Cullen left, Duckett ordered another cup of coffee and tried to put together a plan about how to confront Jetta safely. A meeting at her plantation was too dangerous; Jubal could kill him when he walked through the front door, and no one would be the wiser. There were thousands of places where he could be buried. Next to Rourke, maybe? The safest place was in town, where there would be plenty of witnesses. What about in the judge's office? That would work, and Huckabee was the kind of person who would help to keep Jetta's temper in order. That was sure to erupt when he threatened to spread the news about her son. He sighed and took a drink of coffee. Criminal life was much more dangerous than law enforcement.

9

Chapter Nine: All Cards on the Table

Judge Abner Huckabee had a large and comfortable office on the third floor of the county courthouse. It featured a big oak desk with an oversized marble ash tray, a walnut cigar case and an inkwell with two pens and a bottle of ink. In front of the desk were two leather chairs matched by an oversized, tall leather armchair behind the desk where the judge did his work. Behind the armchair was a bookcase that held a copious number of law books, all of which showed evidence of frequent use. Three large windows took up most of the space on the wall to the right of the desk, assuring that the room was well lit. On the left wall hung a collection of various degrees and honors, in the center of which was a photograph of a class of young law students posing stiffly in black suits and white collars. The back wall held a collection of comic English law prints and a long leather sofa with worn pillows that suggested the judge enjoyed an occasional nap after lunch.

Judge Huckabee and Jetta sat in the judge's office waiting impatiently for the arrival of Parker Kellogg. The judge pulled out his gold watch and consulted it for the third time. "Really, this is most unusual. Kellogg has asked us to meet him here to consider what he calls 'an impressive financial opportunity.' What the devil do you think he has up his sleeve now?"

"I am ready for this meeting," said Jetta. "I think we are finally going to discover exactly who Parker Kellogg really is and what his connection is to Terrance Rourke. I knew that one day I would have to face the consequences for having that devil killed, and today is probably that day."

"There is no way anyone could connect you with Rourke's death! We have covered our tracks too well," argued the judge.

Jetta reached out to him and took his hand. "Old friend, your scheme was absolutely brilliant! But as we all know, 'murder will out,' and I suspect that it is about to happen." At that point, there was a knock on the door, and Kellogg entered the office.

"Miss Jetta, Judge, thank you for agreeing to see me. May I sit down?"

"Sit! Sit! By all means, sit!" said the judge impatiently as he pointed to an empty chair.

Duckett took his seat and placed his hat and a small briefcase on a nearby table. "Let me start by telling you that my real name is Thomas Duckett and I am an investigator for the Pinkerton Company, stationed in Chicago."

"Are we now to understand that you are finally speaking the truth, Mr. Duckett?" asked Jetta sharply.

Duckett flushed and then nodded. "In early February of this year, the company received a special request from a client who asked to meet with me specifically, but who gave a false identity. He wanted to meet with me alone at a local hotel at a given date and time. When I knocked on the door, a voice told me to come in and I walked into a room that was totally dark except for a spotlight that shone into my face and blinded me. The person in the room was behind a tall screen, and I was aware of the smell of a cigar and cologne. The man instructed me to reach under my chair and to remove a document, which was an envelope with a cashier's check made out to me for the sum of five thousand dollars. My client told me he wanted me to go to Pembroke, Georgia and to investigate a plantation there called Heartwood and also the family named Whittlesey, who owned the property. He wanted such details as the physical condition of the property, any financial problems as a result of the war and details on Mr. Champion Whittlesey and his wife, Jetta. I was told that if I did a good job, I would be paid an additional five thousand dollars."

Duckett paused as he asked, "Judge, do you mind if I help myself to a glass of water?" The judge nodded and pointed to a pitcher on the nearby table. Duckett downed a whole glass and then resumed his story. "I learned early that people were slow to give any law officer information, but if you were a buyer of plantation property, they would tell you more than you needed to know. So, I posed as a buyer for a Chicago bank interested in purchasing plantation property in Georgia. Local officials were quite free with their information, especially your local treasurer. Judge, you personally told me the most desirable local plantation was Heartwood, owned by the widow Whittlesey, but insisted that she would never sell the property, despite her financial difficulties."

"Should have kept my mouth shut," grumbled the judge.

"I also attended the local church and befriended Abigail Simpson, where I found out about young Paul and something about his personality."

"Your treatment of Abigail was despicable, and so was your unwarranted intrusion into my family!" said Jetta.

"Unfortunately, this is something we in law enforcement must do regularly, but I swear to you that I always treated Miss Simpson with the utmost respect and never encouraged her to think our relationship was more than friendship."

"When you leave here, remember to call upon her and give her your apologies," said Jetta.

Duckett's face reddened, but he continued. "When I had finished my research, I traveled back to Chicago and met again with my client under the same circumstances as before. He accepted my information with little comment except on two issues. When I reported on Colonel Whittlesey's heroic death, he asked if the colonel had been 'careless with explosives,' which I thought was a rather cruel commentary on a brave officer. I also had a feeling that the colonel's death was something that Rourke already knew about, but I am not sure how.

"The second surprise was his reaction when I mentioned that you had a son named Paul who was five years old. His whole demeanor changed! He wanted to know all about Paul, what kind of boy he was. I told him some of the stories I got from Abigail, and he laughed with delight. It was completely out of character."

Jetta stood up abruptly and said, "I will not listen to any more of this!"

Duckett also stood and stretched out his hand, saying, "Please, Mrs. Whittlesey. I am almost finished. And I think you will find what I have to say is in your and Paul's interest." Jetta reluctantly sat back in her chair.

"When a Chicago newspaper ran a story on Terrance Rourke's disappearance, along with a third of his fortune and his subsequent sighting at an Atlanta train station, I was certain that Terrance Rourke was my mystery client and that he was on his way to Heartwood. My first plan was to contact his family and offer to seek him out for a reward, but to my surprise, neither his business partner nor his wife seemed ready to back such an effort. By leaving his wife with most of his estate and his business partner with a lucrative business, he had guaranteed no interest in searching out his whereabouts.

"I then settled on a new plan. I would find Rourke and tell him I would keep his secret for the sum of $500,000. I realized this plan placed my life in danger, for I knew Rourke would not hesitate to answer my proposal with a bullet to my head. I began my search in Atlanta and with the help of a new associate, I was lucky to discover exactly where Rourke had deposited his money, less a quarter of a million dollars, under the assumed name of Parker Kellogg, the same name I used when I first met with him! He had also given his address as Heartwood Plantation. When I continued my journey to Pembroke, the owner of the stable identified Rourke from his picture in the paper, even though he was clean shaven." Duckett gave a small smile. "Your son Paul labeled him as 'Another Yankee' although I compliment you on your quick response. And finally, when you gave me the tour of Heartwood to clearly show me that Rourke was not living there, I smelled his cologne and cigar smoke in your guest room."

"Rubbish!" said the judge. "You have nothing but a bag of circumstantial evidence no jury would accept!"

"Judge, I am not looking for evidence for a murder trial. I believe it is highly likely that Terrance Rourke is dead and is buried somewhere on Heartwood, and from what I have learned, the world is better off for his loss!" The judge and Jetta looked at him in amazement.

"My associate is older and smarter than me. He also spent some time in the Confederate army. He believes that Rourke headed a group of bummers who raided Heartwood and during that raid, there was some sort of confrontation between him and Mrs. Whittlesey. He thinks that Rourke threatened her that he would burn the property as he was ordered but would spare it if she submitted to his advances. The torch burn in the foyer showed that he was serious.

"Five years later, he was unaware of the birth of Paul until my investigation, but that is why he was so sure Jetta would allow him back into her life, and more to the point, to become a father to Paul. And that is why when he put his money into a bank account, he listed Jetta Whittlesey as co-owner of the money along with himself, but he did not use his real name."

Jetta shook her head in disbelief. "I don't understand."

"Very simple, my dear," said the judge. "If Rourke is dead, if you have proof of who you are, you own a bank account with \$2,750,000. But I assume Mr. Duckett wants part of that money for his assistance."

"My share, including my partner's share, would be a total of one million dollars. You already have \$250,000, so your total would be two million dollars. I think that is quite fair."

"Any bank would want to have proof that the other investor on the account agrees to the disbursement of funds or is deceased," commented the judge.

"I don't see that as a problem," said Duckett. "Rourke was an old and dear family friend who was seriously ill when he visited Heartwood and died of a heart attack. Before he passed away, he informed Mrs. Whittlesey that he was leaving her his estate. I am sure that as a judge, you can prevail upon the family doctor to issue the necessary death certificate."

Jetta laughed bitterly. "You should listen to yourself talk, Mr. Duckett! You sound exactly like Terrance Rourke! If I gave him my body, he would not burn down my home or kill my faithful overseer. Five years later, he reappeared to save Heartwood from creditors if I married him and let him take over the raising of my son! You offer me a fortune if I share it with you and your accomplice, even if such an act would be proof that I had murdered Terrance Rourke. And if I flatly refuse your blackmail, what is my punishment, Mr. Duckett?"

"I… I would be forced to offer the evidence I have collected to the local authorities, including the fact that Rourke was the father of your son," said Duckett.

Jetta stood, picked up her bag and then pulled on her gloves one at a time. She then delivered a powerful slap to Duckett's face, throwing him backwards out of his chair onto the floor. He scrambled to his feet just in time to see her leave the office.

"You had that coming, son," said the judge. "Give her a few days to cool down, and you and I will talk again."

After Duckett had left, the judge sat down heavily in his chair, putting his hands behind his head and pushing back until he was staring at the blank ceiling. After several minutes, he sat upright and walked out of his office, taking a flight of stairs to the offices below and entering one with a plaque that announced Caleb Hightower, Attorney at Law. "Is he here?" he asked the smiling receptionist who rose to greet him.

"Yes, indeed, Judge," she answered. "I will tell him you are here."

"Come in, Abner!" boomed a voice from within. The judge walked into the room and sat himself down in one of two chairs. He looked without blinking at the tall, thin man with curly grey hair, hawk nose and lively brown eyes who stared back at him with a slight smile. "Hmm. Must be something serious," he suggested.

"Caleb, how long have we been friends?"

His friend pretended to think. "Let's see. I came to you when I was nineteen and asked your advice on whether I should join the army or become a lawyer. You convinced me to go to law school, where you were my sponsor, and for two years I served as your law clerk. We probably go back a good thirty years."

"Caleb, I am going to tell you a story that involves a good friend of ours. It is a terrible story. When I finish telling you the story, I am going to ask for your help. I will understand if you cannot help us, but I ask that you keep the information to yourself."

"Just a minute," said his friend. He walked to the door of the office and spoke to his receptionist. "Mildred, I will not be available until I tell you otherwise." He reclaimed his chair and pulled out a drawer where he removed a bottle of whiskey and two glasses. "Now tell me your story."

One hour later, the two men sat silently in the room, drinking their whiskey. Caleb finally broke the silence with a question. "Abner, some of our best talks have centered on whether there is a God or not. You strongly believe there is, and I am less certain. If there is a God, why would he let a fine woman like Jetta Whittlesey face such terrible issues?"

The judge took one last pull on his drink before answering. "Maybe because he knows that men like you and me will come to her assistance."

Hightower nodded. "Good answer," he said. "I am honored you asked for my help. I just need to ask you one question. Do you need a permanent solution to this problem or one that is, shall we say, temporary?"

"If it were my choice, I would want a permanent solution, but I think that would distress Jetta."

Hightower nodded, then stood, revealing the open sleeve on his left arm and offered the judge his right hand. "I will handle the problem," he said.

10

Chapter Ten: Kidnapped

Thomas Duckett sat on the edge of his bed in his underwear, taking small sips from a pint of whiskey he had bought in town. It was dark in his bedroom with a single kerosene lantern providing the only light. The second day of the three-day limit he had given Jetta to respond to his demands had passed without contact, and he was uneasy.

If she listens to the judge, there should be no problem. Hell, she will end up with almost two million dollars she did not even know she had! Terrance Rourke is gone from her life for sure, probably buried in some deep hole on Heartwood. She should be grateful instead of trying to knock my head off!

He tipped the bottle back and let the last of the whiskey burn down his throat and let the empty bottle fall to the floor. He made two swipes at the lantern before managing to turn it off and then fell back on the bed.

He was awakened by something cold pressing on his forehead and he swatted at it in irritation. The pressure lifted momentarily and then was resumed. "Wake up, Duckett. Your worst nightmare is about to begin," said a strange voice.

He groaned and opened his eyes wide and identified the object pressed to his forehead as the barrel of a Colt 45 revolver held by a tall man dressed in white robes with a crimson hood. The left sleeve was noticeably empty. There were two other men dressed in white robes in the room, one who turned up the light on the lantern and another who held a rifle pointed down at Duckett.

Fear seized Duckett by the throat in an iron grip. "Who…who are you? What do you want? Listen, I am a licensed detective. You can't…" The man cocked the weapon without removing it from the Pinkerton man's forehead, and Duckett stopped talking.

"Be quiet! One more word and I will stick your socks down your throat!" The tall man turned to the other two robed figures and pointed with the Colt to Duckett's clothes scattered around the small room. "Gather up his clothes and get him dressed. Tie his hands in front." He pointed to a brown traveling bag in a corner and said, "Pack up all his things. Bring me his wallet and any paperwork you find and any weapons." The men worked quickly and silently handed their leader a leather briefcase and wallet.

"Do you owe Mrs. Barrow any rent?"

Duckett swallowed hard and said, "No, I paid up until tomorrow."

The four men moved quietly through the darkened house and out the back door where four horses were tethered. One man tied a loop in the handle of Duckett's suitcase and hung it on a pommel of his saddle, then helped him to mount his horse. He got on his own horse and reached over to grab the reins on Duckett's mount. "All ready," he said.

Duckett looked about in vain for any sign of help. The night was dark and quiet with only a sliver of a crescent moon reluctantly sharing its light. The few houses they passed had no sign of life, not even an alarm from a curious dog. The group soon turned off the main road and took to narrow trails in the woods where bent branches took stinging swipes at their heads. Duckett clung desperately to the pommel of his saddle to keep from falling off his mount, which shied frequently when the suitcase slapped its flanks.

Finally, they seemed to reach their destination, an abandoned farmhouse whose black glassless windows stared out at the intruders without blinking. Half of the roof had succumbed to gravity and caved in, and the front door clung to its frame by a single hinge. The structure of an old well sat in the front yard, its cover missing several planks.

The man in the red hood swung down off the big grey horse and started giving orders. "Take our guest in the house and sit him down at the table. See if you can find that old lantern and light it up and get a little fire going in the fireplace. Tether the horses and see if you can find a bucket to give them some water." He then removed Duckett's briefcase from the roan's saddlebags and took it into the house.

There was a large hole in the ceiling where water had forced its way to the first floor. The room was illuminated by a rusty lantern that sat on the mantel of the fireplace and a struggling fire fought to survive below. A pile of trash, including broken plates, rags and a decapitated toy bear had been swept into one corner of the room. A sturdy oak table sat in front of the fireplace, its surface showing years of cuts and abuse. Two wooden chairs that had once been green sat at the table, one missing two slats. Duckett was pushed into the chair opposite the fireplace.

The leader sat down at the table and pulled Duckett's notebook out of the leather case. He patted his white robe until he found what he was looking for, then reached into a side pocket and withdrew a black leather eyeglass case. When the man put on a pair of Ben Franklin glasses over the eye slits of his hood Duckett almost burst into laughter until fear overcame his hysteria.

Duckett quickly searched his memory to recall all the information he had recorded in his notebook. The names of the three National banks in Atlanta were there, but he had not identified which one had Rourke's cash. He was sure he had written down his accomplice's name and home address, bur he had not included any information on who he was. Nowhere had he recorded the fictitious name Rourke had used when he opened his account. If he could avoid giving out this information, maybe he still had a chance!

The leader quickly read the information written in the tablet, removed his glasses and slapped the booklet on the table. "Untie his hands," he said. When this was done the leader gave further instructions. "Put both hands on the table, palms down and do not move them an inch!" He lifted the skirt of his uniform and from a leather sheath he slowly removed the largest knife Duckett had ever seen in his life.

"I doubt you have ever seen one of these up north. It's called a Bowie knife, perfected by a famous knife fighter called Jim Bowie, who was killed at the Alamo. Killed a lot of Mexicans before they killed him. Wicked piece of equipment, for sure." He carefully tested the edge of the blade with his thumb, then suddenly plunged it into the table between Duckett's spread hands, which made the Pinkerton man scream and withdraw them quickly.

"Spread your hands back on the damn table and keep them there until I tell you to move!" roared the hooded man. Shaking with fear Duckett slowly put his hands in their original position. The man leaned forward and spoke to him with a low, menacing voice. "Let me tell you what is going to happen today. You are going to tell me the story of the day you went to work for Terrance Rourke until the day you met with Jetta Whittlesey two days ago. Every thought, every act that came in between those days. When you are through, I need to understand every step of your blackmail scheme. It will take a while for me to corroborate what you have told us and if you have omitted one item or told us one lie, when I return, I am going to cut off one finger for every fact you held back. If I run out of fingers I will start on your toes! Start talking!"

An hour later an exhausted Thomas Duckett hung his head in shame. He had revealed the bank where the money was located and the name of his conspirator as well as the false name Rourke had given to the manager. "That is the whole truth, I swear. The result was that Jetta Whittlesey would get more money than she had ever imagined. I meant her and her family no harm."

"No harm except if she refused you would provide the authorities evidence that she had killed Terrance Rourke."

"That was all bluff. What good would that have done us? There is no reward for any information on Rourke from his family or anyone else."

The hooded man stood up and pulled the big knife from the tabletop. "Guess we will never know now, will we? You will be our guest here for a few days while I check out your story. When I return, we will have a serious discussion about your future." He paused a moment. "Assuming that you have one." He gestured to the two other men. "Put him down in the old well and guard him. Find him some food. I will return as soon as I can."

The morning light was starting to replace the dark as the two guards pushed Duckett toward the old well, the taller of the two carrying their captive's suitcase and a stout rope. He put down the case and tied a loop at the end of the rope. "Put this over your head and under your arms and hold on to the rope. Walk your way down the hole in small steps then release the rope when you are on the ground."

Duckett sat on the edge of the well and put the rope over his head and under his arms. He looked back over his shoulder and was relieved to see the bottom of the well was dry. There was a fearful moment as he dangled over the edge, but he pushed off with his legs and found he could walk down the side of the well with ease. The rope was withdrawn and then sent back down with his suitcase. The Klansman looked down into the well and said, "Food and water comin' later tonight," he said. He tossed a small rolled up tarp down to the prisoner, then withdrew.

Duckett sat on his suitcase and took stock of his new home. The well was about twenty-five feet deep and about eight foot in width. The floor was covered with old leaves and small tree branches. An old bucket with a frayed piece of rope attached lay half buried by debris. If the old well cover were put back in place there would be some protection from the elements, but not much. The tarp would come in handy if it rained.

He spread the tarp out on the ground and opened his suitcase, refolding all his clothes and setting them on the tarp. He was happy to see he had packed one heavy jumper. Unfortunately, his pocketknife was missing, but he did find almost a full box of matches, a pint of whiskey and his wallet. His Pinkerton card was missing, but his money seemed intact. Curious.

***

In the old farmhouse, the attorney, Caleb Hightower, had removed his Klan robes and sat at the table while his two henchmen stood. "I left his wallet and his money, so I would guess he will start trying to bribe you tonight. We will be in Atlanta tomorrow, and we soon will have more information. I figure it won't be long before we will have a pretty fair idea of whether we can shut down this blackmail scheme for good or if Jetta is still in some danger."

One of the Klansmen asked, "And if she is?"

Their leader sighed and then shook his head. "Our prisoner may have to take up permanent residency in the well."

***

The next morning Hightower stuck his head into the judge's office. "Reporting for duty, sir!" he announced.

The judge dropped the papers he was reading and pointed to a chair. "Sit! Sit! Tell me what is happening!"

His friend threw himself into a chair, crossed his legs and shook his head. "Abner, this young man is probably a good detective, but be damned if he isn't the worst criminal I have ever seen! He wants to steal some money, but he seems to be loath to hurt anybody in the process."

The judge frowned. "You think he is harmless?"

Hightower shook his head. "I haven't made up my mind yet. Two of my friends and I dressed up in our Klan outfits and picked him up at his boarding house last night. Roughed him up a little bit, and I think he blurted out the whole plan. Gave us the name of his partner in crime, too. A teller at the bank where the money was deposited by Rourke! A banker and a detective! What a fine couple to blackmail our lady friend!"

"Where is Duckett now?"

"Got him stashed in an old well I found on Jetta's property when I was quail hunting. My friends will feed him once in a while and watch him." He looked deep into his friend's eyes and then said, "Told him I would check out his friend and then decide whether I would have to fill in the well or not. I think he believed me."

The judge gave a sigh. "Unfortunately, I believe you, too."

Hightower held up his hand. "Give me some time. It's early yet."

$$11$$

Chapter Eleven: Home Sweet Home

Frances Cullen walked briskly up the lane to the small yellow farmhouse he had inherited from his father and mother. The afternoon had turned warm, and he carried his coat and hat and had loosened his bow tie. His daily trip home included a long trolley ride and a walk through the woods, but he enjoyed his quiet life in the country, accompanied only by his two large yellow cats. He had rented out the farmland to a neighbor, and the income took care of the upkeep.

He removed a large brass key from his pocket and unlocked the white front door, hanging his coat and hat on a hook on the back. He folded back his shirtsleeves and called out to his cats, "Dinner time, kitties!"

"Good! We are starved!" came a voice from his parlor.

Cullen was shocked. He took a few tentative steps and peered around the door. In his favorite armchair sat a tall man in a Ku Klux Klan outfit, scratching the head of one of his cats, who sat contentedly in his lap. His other cat sat on the back of the chair, awaiting his turn. Two men in white outfits stood to the side of the seated man, each carrying a Colt revolver.

"Who are you? What do you want?" blurted Cullen.

The Klansman carefully put each cat on the floor, brushed the hair off his uniform and gestured to one of his men. "See if you can find them something to eat." He then gestured toward an empty chair. "Have a seat, Mr. Cullen. We are here to gather some information about the plan you and Mr. Duckett devised to blackmail Jetta Whittlesey."

Cullen shook his head. "I do not know anyone by those names. You have the wrong person!"

The Klansman shook his head. "I am sorry you choose not to cooperate, Mr. Cullen. But I am sure we can change your mind." He motioned to his men. "Mr. Cullen looks hot after his long walk. Take him out to the horse trough and cool him off."

Cullen tried to flee, but the men grabbed him and bent his arms behind his back. They marched him out to a filled water trough and forced him down to his knees. "When you are ready to talk, give us a signal," said one and then plunged the smaller man's head under the water. Their victim sucked in a huge gulp of air before he was submerged. But quickly bubbles began to surface, followed by violent thrashing of his body. His captors held him for a few seconds, and then he raised a wet arm in surrender. When they stood him on his feet, he leaned over and retched water on the ground. They led him back to his chair and took positions behind him.

The tall Klansman was back in the rocking chair, waiting for him. For the first time, Cullen noticed that his left sleeve was empty and pinned to his uniform.

"Duckett's defense for his actions was that Mrs. Whittlesey knew nothing about the funds Rourke placed in the Atlanta bank, and the fact that he had left them in joint names with no restrictions meant that she could personally withdraw them without anyone making inquiries. He kept saying that she was going to be over a million dollars richer as a result of his plan. Did you agree with that assessment?"

Cullen sneered and shook his head. "My partner knew nothing about how Southern ladies think! Women like Jetta Whittlesey do not accept money from men like Rourke. If that scheme did not work, that's why I suggested threatening to spread the news about Rourke's being Paul's father. That was a much greater threat and one that had a chance of working. I thought there was a fifty-fifty chance of her cooperating and claiming the money for us."

The Klansman was silent for a moment. "What was the other fifty per cent?"

Cullen crossed his arms and stared back at his captor. "That she would have Duckett killed just like she had Rourke killed. That's what happened, isn't it? And you're going to do the same thing to me!"

"That depends on you." The tall man said. He motioned to his two companions, who lifted Cullen from his chair and sat him down at a small oak desk in a corner of the room. The Klansman pointed to some papers lying on its surface. "You will copy what I have written here in your own handwriting and address the envelope to the president of your bank. You confess to sharing information about a client of the bank with Thomas Duckett and conspiring with him to blackmail Jetta Whittlesey for the money. You will claim that you suffered from a fit of remorse and took your own life. I will take the letter and if Mrs. Whittlesey is threatened in any way, you will be found floating in the pond behind your property, and this letter will be lying on your desk. By the way, I have examined your handwriting and your signature on other paperwork on your desk, so be sure your work is accurate. You have a choice: life or death."

Cullen reached for his pen. "I'll do it!"

"Excellent! Then we won't have to find a new home for your cats. One last question before we leave: how much contact will the bank have with their clients with this size of a deposit?"

Cullen shrugged. "That depends on the client. Rourke wanted any interest added to the principal, so there will be no need for cashing interest checks. If the client is satisfied with letting the money sit and draw interest, they will be happy to accommodate him. But if there is no contact for a year or more, they probably will make a personal visit."

"You will discourage that as long as you can."

Cullen shrugged his shoulders. "Of course."

***

"So, what can you tell us about our situation?" demanded Judge Huckabee. "How are we going to eliminate this blackmail threat to Jetta?" The judge, attorney Caleb Hightower and Jetta were back in the judge's office to review the result of Hightower's kidnapping of Duckett and assault on Cullen.

The attorney took a final sip of his tea and put the cup on a nearby table, then returned to his chair. "I am confident that our threats to Cullen—exposing him to his bank and physical threat—have taken him out of the picture. I am thinking about a similar approach to Duckett. Every day he spends down in the well makes him more apprehensive. But the real problem is all that money sitting in that bank in Atlanta, where management has no contact or instructions from the two owners. Eventually, they will come looking, and that's something we must avoid."

Jetta sighed and shook her head. "My situation would be almost comical if it did not threaten my life. I am sitting on a huge pile of money that I do not want, and it could send me to jail!"

"Judge, the best plan is for us to contact the bank before they contact us. Why don't you work on that problem and let me finish with our young detective? We need to put the fear of God into him that he never wants to see this state again. Miss Jetta, I will need to borrow your overseer to help me make my plan work."

"Please be careful! Jubal needs very little incentive to frighten Mr. Duckett permanently!"

12

Chapter Twelve: Death in the Corn Field

"Kneel on your right knee then point your left knee at the target. Good! Now rest your left elbow and your left hand holding the rifle on your left knee, with the gun barrel pointed at your target. Tuck the gun stock into your right shoulder and pick a spot on your target and line it up with the two gun sights on the gun barrel. Don't let your right elbow flop loose, hold it tight against your right side. Perfect! Take a deep breath and let it out, then hold your breath and start squeezing the trigger, gently, very gently. When the gun goes off it should be a surprise to you. There!"

"I hit the target!" said the young boy.

Kneeling beside his younger son Luke, Wilson Lowe grinned and clapped the boy on the back "You sure did! Keep this up and soon you will be as good a shot as your brother Mark!" Lowe took the carbine rifle from his son and helped him to his feet. "Go give the target a push and we'll let Mark have a turn."

Luke scrambled to his feet and ran to the target, a simple wooden cross with a white sheet hanging from a pine tree limb. He gave the scarecrow a push and it began to swing from side to side. Luke ran back to the firing position and Mark stood, side to the target, and began tracing its movement with the gun barrel. When it reached its apex, he fired, and the figure danced into the air. When it came down spinning, he shot again, and the figure spun wildly.

"That's good shootin', young man!"

Lowe spun around and was surprised to see his friend Master Sergeant Festus Taylor and two other soldiers sitting on horseback behind them. "Yo, Sergeant! Didn't know you were in town! Meet my boys, Luke and Mark. Boys, shake hands with the man who saved your daddy's life!"

The big man slowly climbed down from his horse and solemnly shook the hand of each boy, then pointed a thumb at his two companions. "This here's Zeb and Tucker. Tucker's the big fella. They be pretty good shots themselves." He gestured at the two men and said, "Why don't you fellas show the boys some fancy shootin' while I talk with Wilson, here." The two men pulled out their carbines and joined the boys while Lowe and the big man walked out of hearing range. The sergeant threw a heavy arm over the younger man's shoulder and asked, "How you doin' with the politickin'? Think you got 'nough votes to get elected?"

"I feel really good 'bout my chances if we can get a good turnout. That why you are in town?"

"Yeah, got a unit bivouacked outside of town since Monday, sniffin' around, makin' sure the roads are clear so our people can get in to vote. Picked up a rumor the Klan is talkin' 'bout makin' certain you be's the first dead Negro man to run for office." He stopped and looked face to face with his friend. "Election day is only four days off. Why don't you bring your family in to our camp and stay till it's over?"

Lowe shook his head. "We can't let them think they have us scared! If we're free men, we have to act like free men. We'll make out fine."

"Just to make sure, I'm gonna leave my two men with you 'til election day, then they can escort you into town to vote. Wish I had more to spare, but I don't."

"Last time the Klan picked me up, they had about fifteen men. Only real soldier they had was the head man, and I understand he quit. My house got thick walls and hurricane windows. With four good shooters, we should make out fine," said Lowe.

"Them boys in white sheets like to use pine torches to burn down houses with folks inside. That's gonna be your big problem," said the big man.

Lowe nodded, then said, "Lit torches and white sheets make a man a good target. I don't plan to let them get close enough to throw torches on the roof."

Taylor nodded. "Sounds like you got a good plan. He stuck out his hand. "Good luck, son."

Lowe loaded his guns and the two boys on the mule-driven wagon and guided the two soldiers to his house. When the house came into view, he halted the mule and addressed the two soldiers. "Siding made out of thick pine, so are the doors. Windows solid pine, no glass, held out with a stick, locked in place when closed. Two windows on a side, each got a slide-hole to stick a gun through."

The two soldiers exchanged glances. "Looks good," said one. "Corn field in front may give them a little cover."

"That corn field has some surprises for anybody who tries to come through it. Let me drop off the boys and take you over to my neighbor's farm. He got a barn where you can leave your horses so nobody will know you're here. We got a small lean-too in the back where you'll be dry at night. The mule will be fine in the small corral."

"Sounds just like home," laughed one of the men.

"Wait till you eat my wife's cookin'!"

***

That evening Lowe was awakened by a hand shaking his arm. He opened his eyes to see his older son carrying a small candle with a rifle under his arm. "They're here," he said simply. Lowe stuck his feet into his boots and sat up quickly. "How many?" he asked.

"Maybe fifteen, eighteen. They millin' around, lightin' some torches."

Only three small candles were lit, one carried by his son, one on the floor where his wife peered outside through a hole at the back door and one on the floor at the front of the house, where the two soldiers each peered through an opening in the front windows, wearing pants and undershirts only.

"How's the light outside?" asked Lowe.

"Not bad," said the tallest soldier. "We see them a helluva lot better than they can see us. They're linin' up just out of range on horseback carryin' rifles, some with torches. Most probably gonna' open up, see what kinda return fire we got."

"Close the peep holes. Put out the candles. Everybody on the floor, NOW!"

A storm of shots slapped against the front windows and doors, causing the younger boy to cover his ears while the family dog took refuge under the table. The shooting continued for almost ten minutes until it gradually subsided.

"Come on in boys, the coast is clear!" jeered one of the soldiers.

"Probably gonna' rush us with torches to throw on the roof, burn us out. Pick your man but don't fire till I give the order. We fixed up a little surprise for them in the corn field."

Seven riders rushed into the cornfield, their mounts crushing the tall stalks of corn. Their riders screamed threats as they held aloft the burning knots of pine. The yells ended abruptly as five of the men in white were swept from their saddles as if they were hit by a giant scythe as their mounts rushed on without them. The two last riders yanked on their reins to bring their horses to a halt, one horse rearing up to dump his rider to the earth.

"Now! Pick your targets!" yelled Lowe. The first shot threw the surviving rider off his horse still clutching his burning torch. It was swiftly discarded as his foot caught in his stirrup and his horse yanked him through the tall green stalks. The riderless horses drifted away and started chewing on the tall corn. Movement in the stalks indicated some of the Klansmen were still alive.

"What the hell happened out there?" demanded one of the two army sharpshooters.

"Corn is pretty high," said Lowe. "Got me some wood stakes, painted them green, pounded them deep up close to the stalks. Ran some black wire between the stakes. They will take a man's head off if the contact is right."

"Pa! Looks like they're pullin' out!" cried the younger son, who had been looking through the peephole through the front door. Lowe quickly took his place, then frowned as he saw the last white riders pull away. "Too fast for a retreat. They got somethin' else planned." He thought a moment, then yelled, "Back door! Open ground out there and a woods for cover!" The three men rushed to man the peep holes in the back door and windows as shots soon began to pepper the back door. Lowe closed his peephole and crawled over to the tall sharpshooter. "See that oak tree out in front? Got a piece of tin dangling down! Can you spot it?"

The man concentrated carefully on his rifle's sights. "Got it," he said softly.

"Put a couple of shots through it, but not before they charge."

The soldier looked at him and smiled. "You got a bomb out there, doncha?"

"Maybe something more accurate."

A mass of white-coated bodies on foot erupted from the woods, yelling and screaming. Some clutched axes or crowbars, some fired rifles, others carried torches they held high. They had barely cleared the woods when Zeb's rifle shot penetrated a large beehive, sending it crashing to the ground and releasing a swarm of angry bees intent on revenge. No Klansman was spared, and they forgot about their attack on the farmhouse as they tried to defend themselves. The men in the house took their time shooting their enemies as they unsuccessfully tried to run from their buzzing adversaries. A few Klansmen who had hung back in the attack melted away into the woods, leaving a small pile of bodies hosting swarms of black bees.

"Are they gone?" asked Lowe's son Luke.

"Looks like it," said his father. He gestured to the two soldiers and said, "Let's check out the cornfield first and give the bees a chance to settle down. Cora? See if you can round up some bandages." They walked carefully out the front door, their rifles at the ready. In the third row they found a body splayed out on his back, minus the white cape and a neat bullet hole in its forehead.

"My shot," said the tall soldier.

"The hell you say," said his friend." I had him in my sights all the way!"

Two horses stood to one side, peacefully chewing on the fresh corn while their dead riders lay twisted in the furrows. Close by, a grey horse with a broken leg struggled to stand upright with a dead rider in white lying beneath it.

"Damn it! I hoped we would spare all the horses," swore Lowe as he slowly approached the horse and took hold of the reins. The soldier Zeb approached the animal and carefully examined the back leg dangling at an angle. He looked up at Luke and shook his head. Lowe sadly gave the animal one last pat and then quickly shot it behind the ear.

"Over here!" Cried the soldier Zeb. A huge man in white lay on his back between two rows of corn. His hood was missing, showing his red-faced agony and his two hands tried vainly to stop the outpouring of blood from his belly. The man looked up at Lowe and croaked, "Water!" Wilson Lowe kneeled down beside him silently. He knew the man lying at his feet. In his first encounter with the Klan, this man had whipped his bare back raw while Lowe was forced to dig his own grave. He had survived only by a small miracle. The tall soldier shifted his stance. "Not a good idea with a gut wound." Without looking up Wilson said, "He's a goner. Seen enough of them to know." When the water arrived, he took the pitcher, gently raised the man's head and poured some of the liquid into his mouth. The man drank greedily for a moment, then lay back his head, coughed violently, and then died.

"Saw one fella dragged out of the corn by his horse," said Zeb. He covered his eyes and looked around. "There he is! Horse eatin' grass and man still hooked up. Don't seem to be moving." They moved up to the horse slowly, Zeb holding the reins and Lowe unbuckling the stirrup to release the leg slowly, but the man still groaned.

"Leg looks like it's broke, probably more than one place. I'll get Cora to get us some boards and something to wrap it up. Looks like we got five bodies, one survivor, one missing." Luke walked up and joined the other two. "Got one man slashed across the face by the wire, but I think he will make it."

"Full house," said Lowe. "Zeb, go get Cora and tell her what she needs and we'll take a look out back."

When the two men walked around to the back yard, the first thing they saw was a huge axe stuck deep in the back door and beneath it lay a man lying in front of the door. "That one's my fault. He snuck around the side of the house and I didn't see him till the last minute. Thank God for those thick doors!" said Zeb.

Two bodies lay almost overlapping one another. Both had torn off their white outfits and hats almost to the knees.

Lowe looked at Zeb. "What the devil happened here?"

"You never saw anything like it! Those bees got under those funny hats and started crawling and biting their way south. The men went crazy trying to get shed of them."

"Over… over here!" At the edge of the woods, a man was sitting against a tree with a white handkerchief that had turned red tied against his head. He raised his left hand slightly and waved. As the two men approached, the sergeant saw him lift his right arm, which held a large pistol.

"Watch out!" He warned, dropping to one knee and firing three shots at the man, who slumped over.

"Damn! You are quick!" said Zeb.

"Getting good at it," said Lowe. "Third time somebody tried that trick on me."

Tucker came around the corner of the house and joined them. "What' the final count?" he asked.

"Ten dead, two wounded, one dead horse, six live horses, lots of bullet holes in the house, but our side made out fine," said Lowe.

"It's almost light," said Zeb. "We'll take your wagon and load all the dead and wounded it can hold. We can catch two horses and hitch them up to the wagon and tie the rest on the truck 'cept that good-lookin' black stallion. He'll be your new horse. After we reach the camp, we will unload and then bring out a new crew to escort you into town in time to vote and make sure you don't have any more visitors."

"Fine with me, but I also want to get you boys and your boss out here for dinner. We could not have made it without you!"

13

Chapter Thirteen: Election Day

Wilson Lowe felt a surge of confidence as he awoke on election day. His last appearance three nights ago at a large Negro church had been well received, and most of the congregation had remained after his speech to shake his hand and to offer him promises of support. He was impressed by their understanding of the important issues of the day and by their determination to vote despite the danger of possible attacks by the Ku Klux Klan. After yesterday's battle, it did not appear that the men in white would be much of a problem for a while. When he threw his blanket off and swung his legs out of bed, he noticed a black suit draped on a nearby chair, with a white note pinned to the lapel. "Good Luck to our new Congressman," it said and was signed by Joe Feeney. He slipped on the coat and found it to be a perfect fit.

He lathered his face and shaved more carefully than usual, polished his boots and dressed in the new suit and his best shirt. When he walked downstairs into the large family room, he found his wife and two boys waiting for him with a round of applause and a sign on his chair saying, "Good Luck, Congressman Lowe." Breakfast was a joyous affair, and his eyes misted over as he recalled his life as a field hand, then a Union soldier, a small landowner and family man and finally, his opportunity to serve as a representative of his people for the state of Georgia. God had been good to him.

"The soldiers arrived about an hour ago," said Cora, his wife. "Zeke and Tucker are outside groomin' your new horse." His younger son said, "His name is Blaze! They let me get up on him and give him a carrot!"

When Lowe walked outside, the two soldiers were just finishing their work, and the big stallion's coat was shining in the sunshine.

"Good morning, men! That's a beautiful animal. Who owns him?"

"Good mornin', Congressman! Blaze belongs to you. Master Sergeant Taylor confiscated the horses of every man he found who joined in the attack. This horse belonged to a man named Bubba Awford. He was the big fella with the axe at the back door."

"Did the sergeant arrest any more Klansmen?"

"Yeah, he was smart! Went around to Doc Jordan's house and he found a bunch of men being treated for bad bee stings. Charged every last one of them!"

***

When he reached the center of town with his escorts, Lowe was shocked by the size of the turnout. The small building that housed the Democratic Party office was overwhelmed with supporters shaking hands and clapping backs. A uniformed brass band kept the mood lively and upbeat. Two years earlier, the Democrats had decided to boycott the election and had given the Radical Republicans a free rein, but this year the party smelled a victory and urged everyone to vote. There was a respectable crowd of Negro supporters in front of the Republican headquarters but very few white people.

Wilson Lowe spotted his friend Sergeant Taylor and a group of Negro soldiers gathered quietly a block away from the activity and made his way over to the group. "What is going on? Looks like the Republicans have ceded the election."

"You ain't heard, I guess. Yesterday, the committee investigatin' Governor Bullock started talkin' about findin' him guilty on charges of fraud. He musta seen it comin' 'cause he took off like a jackrabbit and left the state, says he is comin' back though. Nobody knows where his money man, Kimball is either."

"What about our county vote? Did we have a large enough turnout to win some seats in the House?"

"Gonna' be close. I saw some of our people turn around and go home after they heard about what the governor did. Top of everything else, yo' party chairman tried to sneak some no-good Negroes in from a train with false papers. We caught 'em 'fore they got off the train, kicked their ass back where they belong."

Lowe joined a group of Negro voters waiting in line, forcing himself to put on a smile and a positive attitude. Many of his people encouraged him to persevere in his quest and to join in an effort to come up with a new slate of respectable Republican candidates before the next election. He waited in line until he had voted then left to go home to share the bad news with his family.

"Sergeant Lowe?"

Lowe recognized the voice even before he turned around, even though he did not recognize the tall, well-dressed stranger with the empty left sleeve. "Yes, sir," he said. "They didn't arrest you, I am glad to see."

"They did not. I had resigned from the Klan the same night I turned you loose and the word got around fast. So, I owe you one."

Lowe shook his head. "I think we are more than square, sir."

The tall man extended his right hand. "Colonel Caleb Hightower. I understand you won a decisive victory last night with a few good shooters and a big company of bees."

Lowe returned the handshake. "You know how the system works, sir: Use anything that works!"

The attorney reached into his pocket and produced a calling card, which he offered to Lowe. "Lowe, I hope you remain active in politics. This country needs men like you if we want to succeed as a nation. If I can help you with your efforts, please call on me. I voted for you today, and I am happy to tell my friends why I did so." He gave a small smile. "I may even convince you to run on the Democratic ticket! Right now, you have a lot more in common with us than that sorry bunch of Republicans we just kicked out of office."

***

The next afternoon, Lowe went back into town to check on the final vote count, which was posted on a bulletin board at the local post office. The Democrats had won every seat in the county handily, but he was the top vote getter for the Republicans. He took small consolation from that and walked down a half block to the Republican headquarters. The large Vote Republican! sign hung down over the porch, held by a single cord, and campaign literature was scattered everywhere. Inside, chairs and tables were in disarray, and the room was dark. A "Victory Bar" of various whiskies was largely untouched, and flies circled over the untouched foods.

"Congratulations, Champ! You were our top vote getter. I even voted for you myself, and I am not even a resident!" Joe Feeney sprawled in a chair tilted back against the wall. His legs were crossed on the top of a small table, and an uncorked Scotch bottle dangled from his right hand. He made a motion toward the bar. "Help yourself."

"Little early for me," He righted a chair and sat down in front of the big Irishman. "So, what do we do now?"

Feeney removed his feet from the table and stood up. He put the bottle on the table and reached out to envelop Lowe's hand with his huge paw. "By God, I knew that's what you were going to say! I knew it! What we are going to do is start all over from page one. We find the best people we can find, white and Negro. We put together a platform that helps both the rich and the poor and kicks all the scallywags and carpetbaggers out on their asses! We tell 'em how hard it is gonna' be but how good its gonna' be when we finish!" He wagged a finger at Lowe. "And we only steal what we need to live, no more!"

"You were doin' good there 'til the end."

Feeney sat down heavily in his chair, took a pull on the bottle, then pointed it at the Negro man. "Now, you may have another choice, believe it or not."

Lowe was curious. "And what is that?"

"Negro Americans owe their freedom and their new-found rights to President Abraham Lincoln and the Republican Party, no question about that. But it was the Radical wing of the Republican party that made your freedom a reality, especially the Abolitionists, who saw your slavery as a moral challenge. The rest of the Republican party went along for the ride and because they needed Negro labor for the cotton industry to survive. When the war ended, the Democrats tried to turn back the clock and return things to the way they were, but the Radicals responded by sending the Union Army back to put Yankees in charge of state government and insist on execution of the new amendments. But now the country is tired of the war and tired of the bickering. Slowly but surely, the Democrats are working their way back into power and they are getting used to Negro freedom. In the long run, it is the new Democratic Party that you are going to have to deal with. And it is easier to do that from the inside than outside."

The sergeant shook his head. "That's hard for me to believe."

"In the state of Georgia, the Democrats outnumber the Republicans in every county except those in the cotton belt where the plantations are concentrated, but that is changing daily. Negroes are being lured into other counties by the demand for labor to rebuild industries and repair the railroad. Money talks and labor walks. Take my word for it as an old, experienced politician; one day the Negro people in Georgia will embrace the Democratic Party. And so will you!" He stood up and enveloped the smaller man in a big hug. "And if you cross over, I cross over too!"

14

Chapter Fourteen: All the World's a Stage

At four in the afternoon, Caleb Hightower ran up the stairs from his office to where Jetta and Judge Huckabee waited for a report on his trip to Atlanta. He was in high spirits and held a bag carrying a bottle of French burgundy and three glasses. He smiled at the judge's secretary without stopping, placed the bag on the floor while he opened the door to the judge's office, then kicked it closed with his heel.

"Good afternoon, friends! I bring you good news and a reason to celebrate our first step in our plan to remove the threat to our friend Jetta Whittlesey!" He placed the bag on Judge Huckabee's desk, reached in his pocket for a corkscrew and placed it beside the bag. "Judge, will you do us the honors?"

Jetta clapped her hands. "How wonderful! I am so in need of some good news for a change!"

Hightower pulled up a chair and proceeded to give them a lively account on the raid on Frances Cullen's house, including the dunking in the horse trough and his two cats. "When we left him, he was convinced that we had killed his friend Duckett and would kill him if he caused us any trouble! So, we were successful with Jetta's wish that there would

111

be no bloodshed in our plans."

He took a sip of wine, then got up from his chair to pace around the room. "While I was at Cullen's house, I was suddenly aware of how the situation was like a performance at a theater, a performance so well executed that the audience believed it was real! So, now our first chapter is over and the curtain falls."

"And the audience rises to its feet with an ovation," said the judge." But what happens in the second act?"

"The plot is much the same, but the costumes change and we have a new leading man, a man that Thomas Duckett fears more than anyone else."

Jetta frowned. "Who would that be?"

Hightower took another sip of wine and paused for effect. "Jubal," he finally said.

"That's too dangerous! Jubal is more than ready to kill Thomas Duckett in real life, not in a play!" exclaimed Jetta.

"That is what will make his performance so believable. I need to come to your home tonight to give him a lesson so he will be fully aware of what we need to do, and you need to be there as well. We do not have a lot of time for practice. The curtain goes up tomorrow night."

***

Thomas Duckett had done his best to make his new living accommodations bearable. He had used the old, rusted bucket to dig a deep hole that served as his commode. Nights he slept sitting on his suitcase, back against the dirt wall, wrapped in the rubber poncho. He used a tiny bit of each day's water supply and some soap from his shaving kit to shave, which made him feel better. The arrival of his one meal was the highlight of the day, as well as a chance to talk to another human being for a few moments. So, when the shadows began to fill the well cavity and no man in white appeared, he began to grow apprehensive. When a shadow finally blocked the light, he was relieved.

"Hello! I thought you had forgotten me! What's for…"

It was not one of the Klansmen looking down into the well, but Jubal, Jetta's massive overseer, who silently looked down at the captive with folded arms. "Klan men, they tell Miss Jetta they kill you tonight, jus' like 'yo partner, no need to feed you no more. Bury you where you is."

Duckett staggered backward and sat on the suitcase hard. "What… what are you doing here?"

"Miss Jetta, she tells me, come here, pull you out of hole, put you on next train to Savannah. Give me some clean clothes. Tie de rope to yo' suitcase, t'ro it up here."

Duckett tied the rope around the handle of the suitcase and tossed the coiled end to Jubal. He untied the suitcase and dropped the rope back into the well. "Tie rope 'round 'yo waist."

Duckett hesitated. He knew Jubal hated him for the danger he presented to Jetta. Was he the rescuer or the executioner?

Jubal gave a nasty laugh. "You want to stay in hole, wait for Klan? I tell Miss Jetta."

When he turned away Duckett cried, "Wait! Wait!" and hurriedly tied the rope around his waist. The big Negro man hoisted him up effortlessly then handed the Pinkerton man a bundle of clean clothes, an old towel and a bar of soap. "River dis way," he said. Duckett picked up his suitcase and followed him to the river's edge. Between what he had in the suitcase and the clothes Jubal brought he put together a clean outfit. He found his shaving kit and hung his small mirror on a nearby tree, lathered his face and then began to shave. When he finished, he stripped off his clothes, grabbed the bar of soap and strode gratefully into the cool water, washing his whole body. After a brisk rub down, he put on his new clothes and felt some of his confidence return. He was not going to die tonight, and he soon would be free again.

"Jubal," he said. "Why can't you put me on the train to Atlanta. I can catch a train direct back to Chicago."

The big man nodded. "I hopes you do dat. Klan got yo' detective card, knows where you works at, knows what you do, where you live. No time, they find you and I no worry' bout you no more. Chicago big city. Plenty of big holes dere."

Duckett's new confidence shriveled. His plan to change his life by claiming some of Rourke's fortune had backfired completely, costing him his job, his secure lifestyle and his future. He would spend the rest of his life on the run, constantly looking over his shoulder.

The hunter was now the hunted.

Jubal brought up the mule cart, and Duckett loaded his suitcase in the back and got up on the front seat with him. He reached into his pocket and gave Duckett an envelope. "Yo ticket" he said and slapped the mule with the reins.

When they reached the station, the train was waiting, ready to depart. The conductor was walking up and down its length, looking at his watch. Smoke was billowing out of the stack. Duckett started to jump down when Jubal grabbed his arm with a painful grip. "Don' come back," he said. Duckett pulled away, grabbed his bag and ran to the train. He gave the ticket to the conductor and hastened on board, flopping into a seat by the window where he could still see Jubal. The train made its first lurch and began to move.

Suddenly, Duckett saw two men running for the train. Jubal looked over his shoulder and saw them too. He grabbed both of them in his big arms as they fought to get free, and one of them finally broke loose and ran after the train. Duckett looked on aghast as the man tried to jump on the train, but it was moving too fast. He finally stopped, made a gun out of his thumb and finger and pulled the mock trigger. Duckett fell back in his seat with horror. An old lady sitting in front of him on the next seat turned around and looked at him, then moved to a seat farther away.

As the train rolled out of view, Caleb Hightower walked out of the station office, puffing on a cigar and clapping his hands. "Well done, gentlemen!" he said to Jubal and the two men who had guarded Duckett. "Very realistic!"

"Been better if I had a real gun," said one man.

Jubal was still watching the train as it disappeared. "Tru dat!" he said.

15

Chapter Fifteen: All's Well That Ends Well

Caleb Hightower looked out the window in Judge Huckabee's office, his right hand in his pants pocket. "My friends, we have come to the last chapter in our drama." He walked away from the window and began pacing the floor. "I am certain that neither of our two villains presents a threat to us anymore. But unfortunately, our greatest concern still lies with us: the money in the bank identified as owned by Jetta Whittlesey and the late Terrance Rourke, posing as Parker Kellogg. Unfortunately, the bank knows what Rourke looks like, where he was going and the name of the lady he planned to meet at this address, although his arrival would be a shock to her."

Caleb leaned over the back of a chair. "Jetta wants no part of this tainted money, which is to her credit. Unfortunately, without her knowledge, she was identified as an associate owner to the bank. Since there will be no activity in the account with Rourke dead, eventually the bank will send a representative to the plantation to seek out Rourke, alias Kellogg, as their primary contact. If the man is not at Heartwood and Jetta has no information about his whereabouts, it is highly likely the bank will report his absence to the local authorities, which is precisely what we must avoid.

"I propose that we anticipate that action with a proposal to the bank that will satisfy everyone, including Jetta and will eliminate any chance of her being charged with Rourke's demise. This will be the final curtain of our performance and it will require two new characters for our play."

"Who will that be?" asked Jetta.

"This will be the climax of our production, my dear! It must be you, attended by your friend, the judge."

***

Three days later the judge and Jetta stood before the entrance to the First National Bank of Atlanta, after a long train ride from Heartwood. Jetta looked stunning in an all-black ensemble, black gloves and a small black hat with a matching black veil. She carried a thin, black, furled umbrella. The judge wore his best suit, with a yellow vest displaying a gold watch chain and a homburg hat.

"Are we ready to begin our performance?" asked the judge.

Jetta pulled back her shoulders. "Up with the curtain," she said.

The judge removed his homburg and gave a slight bow as he held open the brass door. "After you, madam!" he said.

The woman who burst through the door exuded power and determination, her shoulders back and her head erect. She marched up to the formally attired greeter and demanded, "Francis Cullen, please. He is expecting me."

When Cullen looked up from the paperwork that had his attention, he was confronted by a tall woman in a black dress scowling at him. He stood up hastily and said, "Good day, madam. I am Francis Cullen. How can I be of service?"

With one sweep of her umbrella, Jetta sent the collected papers on Cullen's desk flying. "I know well who you are, you miserable little man! You were Thomas Duckett's partner in a wicked scheme to blackmail me! Mr. Duckett underestimated his victim, and it was injurious to his health." She leaned closer to the cowering chief teller and asked, "And how is your health, Mr. Cullen? Is it in jeopardy? Do you still live alone in that little yellow house in Shepherd's Valley?" She paused. "With your two yellow cats?"

Cullen was a smart man, but he struggled to absorb an overload of information. The first was the use of the past tense verb in connection with his partner in crime. Second, their victim was threatening him, and she knew not only where he lived but some other personal details. Most importantly, she exuded a sense of power that left no doubt that she was capable of executing the threat she was issuing. He was struck dumb. Jetta glared at him for a few seconds then turned on her heel and stomped out of his office. She gestured imperiously to the greeter, who had returned to the front door and heard none of her diatribe. "I am Mrs. Champion Whittlesey, and I have an appointment with your general manager, Wilson Makepeace."

Mr. Makepeace came out from behind his desk to take Jetta's hand and give her a slight bow. "Welcome, welcome, Mrs. Whittlesey. I am pleased to meet one of our most important customers. Please be seated."

Jetta gracefully sat in one of the chairs and began removing her gloves. "Mr. Makepeace, this is Judge Abner Huckabee, a long-time friend and my attorney."

Makepeace leaned forward to shake the judge's hand. "Welcome, sir." He looked around and asked, "Will Mr. Kellogg not be attending our meeting?"

The judge held up a finger. "Before we address that issue, I think it is important that we establish our bona fides." He reached into a black briefcase and extracted a single letter, which he handed to the bank manager. "This letter from the president of Savannah National Bank, an old friend of mine, confirms my identity and that of Mrs. Whittlesey as one of his current clients. And here is a copy of Mrs. Whittlesey's birth certificate."

"Thank you, but that is quite unnecessary."

The judge removed a newspaper clipping from his case and passed it to the banker. "Is this the man who deposited two million, seven hundred fifty thousand dollars in your bank last April in a joint account with Mrs. Whittlesey?"

The bank president took the clipping and read it carefully before nodding. "Yes, this is the man who identified himself as Parker Kellogg and who established a joint account with Mrs. Whittlesey. In fact, a Pinkerton detective showed me the same information and wanted information about the money." He shook his head and said, "It is not unusual for our customers to use fictitious identification. The detective had no evidence of any crime committed by the depositor, and I refused to answer any of his questions. If I remember correctly, the paper gave his real identity as Terrance Rourke, a wealthy Chicago businessman."

"Shortly after Mr. Rourke visited your bank he made a completely unexpected appearance at Heartwood, my plantation," said Jetta." I had not seen him since an incident that occurred in 1865, toward the end of the Civil War. A raiding party of General Sherman's troops raided Heartwood for provisions for their troops and animals, led by an officer and Rourke, who was then a sergeant. The officer left with another group of raiders after ordering Rourke to burn the plantation when he had finished."

"I worked feverishly to rescue as many things from the house as possible. When they were ready to leave, the sergeant lit a torch and escorted me into the house. He dropped the torch on the floor, let it burn for a moment and then, to my astonishment, threw a small rug on the flames and extinguished the fire! He told me that I was a brave woman and he could not bear to burn such a lovely property and to tell anyone who asked that I had been able to put out the flames after the raiders left! Two years later, I was surprised to receive a letter from him, postmarked Chicago. He said that he was married and had a very successful business and wondered if I and the plantation had survived the war. I answered with a short letter thanking him again for his efforts, and that was the last I had heard from him.

"What an incredible story!" said the banker.

"It got even more incredible when Rourke appeared on my front porch with no warning! I almost did not recognize him, he was so well-dressed and confident! He said that he had heard that Heartwood was about to be sold for unpaid taxes in a few days and he had decided he could not allow that to happen. He showed me a valise full of greenbacks and told me there was enough money there not only to pay the taxes but also to settle any debt with my factor! In fact, he insisted on taking me to the tax office the very next morning! When we returned, I made him sit down with me and explain how he had decided to come to my assistance again when we barely knew each other and had separate lives and families.

"Please understand me. I had no feeling I was talking to a man who was deranged or suffering from some mental illness. He had given considerable time to development of his plan, and he had absolute confidence in its success! He said that making money was child's play for him and he now found it boring. He had married well and had three daughters in the hope of finally having a son, but that had not happened. He had decided to embark on a new life, with a new name, in a new area of the country, with a new wife. First, he had made sure that one half of his fortune went to his wife and daughters and that his business was in order. Then he made a very effective disappearance, except for a business acquaintance who recognized him in the Atlanta train station."

The banker nodded. "I agree that the man I knew as Parker Kellogg was in complete control of himself. He was brusque, confident, even a bit rude when negotiating for his interest rate. Still, how could he presume you would be agreeable to such an arrangement without some form of…of…"

"Some form of encouragement from me?" suggested Jetta.

"Well…yes!"

"I think Terrance Rourke was one of the few men in this world who was always successful in getting what he wanted. Sometimes it took brute force, sometimes money, sometimes persuasion. Unfortunately for him, he set his sights on a woman who had a perfect life before losing her husband in the war. But she still has the memory of his love, a young son to raise and a fine plantation that needs attention. I have no room for another man in my life."

"Mrs. Whittlesey, we seem to be referring to Mr. Rourke in the past tense. Has something happened to the gentleman?"

"Yes indeed! Something tragic! The day after we returned from the bank, he asked if he could meet my son and perhaps take him for a buggy ride around the plantation with me. I agreed, provided that I went along. Well, it was a fine day and we had a splendid time. He and my son Paul got along just fine. When we returned, he praised my son and told me that with the money he was going to leave me, I could give Paul the finest education money could buy, and he would raise the boy as if he were his own son. I told him I was very grateful for the money he had given me, but that I would treat it as a loan and would pay it back in monthly installments. I also said I had no desire to marry again. He said he understood but that he had already deposited money for me at your bank and that I could do with it what I wanted. After dinner that evening, he took a bottle of whiskey out on the porch and said he understood it would be a full moon and wanted to see it." She shook her head and began to cry, and the judge handed her his handkerchief.

"A maid found him the next morning, still sitting in the chair. He had killed himself with a small derringer I did not know he had."

The judge handed two documents to Makepeace. "There is the death form from our local doctor and a letter from the sheriff confirming the suicide."

"What does the bank do with the money?"

The judge finally entered the conversation. "My understanding of a joint account is that both parties must sign an agreement in the presence of an officer of the bank."

"Well, yes, technically that is correct, but either party can endorse it later."

"The other party has no interest in signing such a document, as you have just witnessed. My suggestion is that you have the bank's attorney locate Mr. Rourke's attorney in Chicago. I am sure Mr. Rourke has a will that would indicate what his plans were for his estate. I would like to know what the final outcome is, of course and that satisfies Mrs. Whittlesey's wishes."

The banker stood up and shook Jetta's hand. "Mrs. Whittlesey, you are an extraordinary woman. We will endeavor to do exactly what you have asked."

***

They paused outside the bank as Jetta pulled on her gloves. "Well, Judge, what do you think?"

"My dear, your performance was flawless! I think you have just removed the only evidence that would make a jury convict you of manslaughter. Congratulations!"

16

Chapter Sixteen: The Journey

Hamilton, the chief doorman of the prestigious Palmer House in Chicago, prided himself on being an expert on people, especially the many guests he welcomed to his kingdom. This talent enabled him to stay one step ahead of his charges in anticipating their every need for making their visit a success. Their satisfaction was then expressed by the discreet exchange of folded greenbacks that allowed him to live a comfortable life.

For example, take the tall, dark, stunning woman slowly alighting from one of the horse-drawn cabs that serviced the railroad terminal. While a valet in a red tunic with brass buttons attended to her luggage, Hamilton doffed his top hat and took her hand as she departed the coach.

"Good morning, madam, and welcome to the Palmer House! My name is Hamilton, and I am pleased to assist you with any of your needs during your visit."

"Good morning, Hamilton! I am Mrs. Champion Whittlesey. What an elegant hotel! I have looked forward to my stay here."

Ah, the lovely, slow cadence of a Southern lady of quality! Maybe one of the Carolinas? A woman who spends a lot of time outdoors, judging by the tan, perhaps on a plantation? Lovely diamond ring, so she is married but traveling alone, which is rare, so perhaps she is a widow. The dress is well made but out of fashion, with no "bustle-bump" on its rear. So, this is not a woman of high fashion. In any case, she is a lone woman in an unfamiliar city, and I will see to her comfort and safety while she enjoys our city.

"Will you need any assistance with transportation while you are here, Mrs. Whittlesey?"

The lady opened her bag and removed a card which she passed on to Hamilton. "I have a very important meeting at this address tomorrow afternoon. Can you make the travel arrangements for me?"

Hamilton looked at the address and said, "Indeed I can, madam! Your coach will be right here tomorrow at one o'clock. Your trip should take a little less than an hour. A very nice sector of Chicago with lovely homes."

Jetta thanked him and discreetly handed him a folded greenback, which magically disappeared, and he walked her to the front entrance and held the door open. Once she entered, Jetta stopped short, impressed by the beautiful, long lobby. Massive columns were lined up down the front walls, holding up a curved ceiling that featured embedded artwork of every description. The columns and the ceiling carried the latest bright "electric" lights that were all the fashion. The hard marble floor was softened by large, colorful, oriental rugs and large leather chairs and sofas, their backs protected by ornate, white linen antimacassars.

Jetta walked to the front desk, followed by the young man carrying her two bags. "Good morning! I am Mrs. Champion Whittlesey, and I have a reservation."

"Good morning, Mrs. Whittlesey, and welcome to the Palmer House. You have come a long way to visit us."

"Indeed, I have. This is my first trip north, and I am amazed at the size and variations of this country. And how busy everyone seems to be! Buildings seem to be springing up everywhere, especially here in Chicago!"

"Wait until you tour Chicago, ma'am! Since we opened the new canal that links us with the Great Lakes, we have become one of the fastest-growing cities in the world!"

"Maybe tomorrow. I think I am ready for a short nap."

"There is a menu in your room, ma'am. If you would like a light lunch later, just pick up your telephone and call our dining room."

"Good heavens! My own telephone! How exciting!"

Her valet, who had a badge that listed his name as Steven, picked up her bags and said, "This way, ma'am," and walked until he turned a corner and stopped in front of a series of double doors where a few people were waiting. Jetta suddenly realized she was about to experience her first elevator ride! She hesitated a moment, then entered the lift, which was operated by an older gentleman in a dark blue uniform.

As the elevator took off, he leaned over and whispered, "First ride?"

"Yes!" she whispered back. "Don't tell anyone!" and he shook his head.

Her room was lovely, with plenty of light, an enormous bed and a wide, inviting tub. There was a vanity mirror with a table full of every conceivable kind of toiletry. She walked over to one of two large windows and parted the curtain to view the impressive sight of the city of Chicago at work.

"Oh, Champion! How I wish you were here with me! What a wonderful time we could have had, exploring this great city!" She closed the curtains, slipped out of her dress and shoes and collapsed on the big bed. She woke with a start, checked her watch and hurried to bathe and dress for dinner.

"Good evening, madam. My name is Charles, the maître d'. Are you dining alone? This way, please." He seated her at a table and gave her an imposing menu card.

"My goodness! What an array of wonderful choices! What do you suggest?"

"Ah! You are dining in the city that claims to offer the most delicious beef in the world, even better than Texas. Let me order for you."

Her waiter arrived with a wine glass and a carafe of French burgundy. "With the compliments of the hotel, madam."

The wine was superb, the steak outstanding and the vegetables new and different. When she finished, Charles examined the clean plate and nodded his approval. He waved to a waiter carrying a full tray that turned out to be a selection of French pastries.

"Charles, I couldn't! I am full!"

"Please, madam! Our chef is very sensitive!"

***

Back in her room, Jetta sat on the bench and combed her long hair. She put down the brush and looked at her reflection in the large mirror. You have had one of the best days of your life, my dear, at the hands of some nice people who do not even know you. Remember this day and cherish it, for tomorrow you have one of the most terrible duties to perform you have ever known.

***

The next afternoon Jetta's coach was waiting just as Hamilton said it would. "Your driver is Norman, Mrs. Whittlesey. He is an excellent driver and knows Chicago like the back of his hand. He will stay with you as long as you need him. It's a bit cool, so I put a blanket in the back."

"Thank you, Hamilton." She impulsively reached out and gave him a hug. "You people here have been so kind to me!"

Progress was slow at first, because the traffic was so heavy, but it thinned out as they got further into suburban Chicago. The houses that started small grew larger and more expensive, and the commercial buildings disappeared. Finally, her driver pulled up in front of a large stone house with an expansive lawn. It was also surrounded by a tall black metal fence that Jetta had not counted on. After she sat silent for a while, Norman turned and asked, "Would you like me to ring, ma'am"?

"No, Norman, thank you. I will do it myself."

He helped her down, and she walked up the road to the fence, where she saw a black bell, which she rang. Shortly, a tall man in a butler's outfit came out the front door, down the steps and approached the fence. "Can I be of service?" he asked.

"I am Mrs. Champion Whittlesey, and here is my card. I have made a long trip from Georgia to contact Mrs. Terrance Rourke and to bring her news about her husband. I hope that she will see me."

The man returned quickly and said, "Please come in, Mrs. Whittlesey." When Jetta entered the house and walked into the foyer, a tall, thin lady with white hair dressed in a simple black dress came forward with her hand extended. "I am Isabelle Rourke, Mrs. Whittlesey. Come into the next room where we can talk. I have a fire lit." They settled in matching armchairs on either side of the fireplace.

"I was not surprised when Terrance left us, and I knew better than to try and find him. He left us with a fine business and a good manager and enough money to live comfortably. Ours was not a love marriage, but he was good to me and the girls, even though he was quite disappointed I could never give him the son he wanted. I took care of Terrance, and he took care of me, but we were never close. He never chased after any woman, but increasingly I knew that somewhere he had a woman that he loved and eventually would try to find her. I thought the only way I could find out what happened to him was if that woman came to tell me the truth. And here you are."

"Mrs. Rourke, I have sad news for you and your children. Terrance Rourke is dead. And I must confess to you that I am the one who had him killed. To this day, I believe he gave me no other choice."

"That does not surprise me. Tell me your story."

About the Author

Patrick Cavanaugh is a native of the Eastern Shore of Maryland, the author of many short stories about its culture and people. He is a graduate of Williams College, an Air Force veteran and was a Ford dealer for many years. His first novel, *Beneath the Quince Bush,* came out in 2019.

Also by Patrick Cavanaugh

Beneath the Quince Bush

Georgia architect Hugh Whittlesey is proud of the restored Heartwood plantation, home of five generations of the Whittlesey family, including the late Confederate Medal of Honor Colonel Champion Whittlesey and his lovely wife Jetta. When the decapitated body of decorated Union Sergeant Terrance Rourke is found buried in the garden at Heartwood, Hugh supports the investigation by detective Arlene Fulbright and her partner. But as the trail of evidence reveals that the victim was murdered not during his Civil War raid of the estate, but after the war's end, Hugh realizes the investigation could have serious implications for his own family and for his distinguished forebearers. Why did Rourke abandon his Chicago family and much of his post-war fortune to return to Heartwood, and who killed him there? Follow the story through the perspective of both the present and the past as it traces the consequences of Sherman's "March to the Sea" for the Whittlesey family.

www.ingramcontent.com/pod-product-compliance
Lightning Source LLC
Chambersburg PA
CBHW071128100726
47908CB00008B/2532